For My Go
Friend Marcia Stern —
Always Keep Your Chin Up!

Jean Johnson
4/09

Mystery House

Written by
Fran Johnson

Artwork by
Francis Sargent

authorHOUSE®

AuthorHouse™
1663 Liberty Drive, Suite 200
Bloomington, IN 47403
www.authorhouse.com
Phone: 1-800-839-8640

First published by AuthorHouse 11/14/2008

ISBN: 978-1-4389-3153-1 (sc)
ISBN: 978-1-4389-3152-4 (hc)

Printed in the United States of America
Bloomington, Indiana

This book is printed on acid-free paper.

**This book was written for
and is dedicated to
a young man that I admire and
love very much, my grandson,**

Brandon Scott Johnson

I want to give special thanks to my dear friend,
Amy Acosta Johnson, without her help this book would
never have been published. Thank you Amy, you are a dear.
May God continue to bless your life.

CHAPTER ONE

CALEB LEARNS THE JOY OF HELPING

It was one of those hot, sweltering days the south is known for and Chip, who was a big, brawny fellow, was doing his best to get an area on his lot laid out and formed up so that he could pour a cement foundation that afternoon. Between the heat of the day and the sweat pouring into his big brown eyes, he could tell that the task was not going to be completed without someone's help. Just then he spotted his eleven-year-old nephew dashing from his house next door with a basketball in his hand. "Hey Caleb, how's about given Uncle Chip a helping hand?"

"Yes, sir," he drawled, "but whatcha trying to do?"

"Well, I've got a small task. A…at least I thought it was a small task. But once I got started I saw right away that I needed another pair of hands and a strong back to help me. And you know I've seen how good you can swing a baseball bat! So, well…my expectations are that you can handle a shovel just as good, do you think?"

"Don't know, sir, but I'm sure willing to try. How's about showing me what we're doing and I'll help ya the best I can."

"Whew! Son, you're an angel in disguise. Look over here; see where I have these stakes with the string tied between them? We need to level the ground in this area from the front here to the back over there. Now here in the front it is twelve feet across and it is nice and flat but then it starts slopping upwards toward the back stakes. Those back stakes are about ten feet away, so what you and I need to do is dig out the soil on the slope until it is even with the front part."

"I'll help but I've never done this much digging before. All I've ever done is help my Dad with the flower gardens around the house. Just let me get some gloves from the garage and I'll get started," Caleb said as he ran off toward his house.

Caleb was a bright, very alert young lad who had always been willing to lend a hand to any one who asked for help. So folks referred to him as a little man because he acted so adult-like. He always grinned from ear to ear and his blue eyes had a special twinkle in them. You didn't know for sure if it was because he was so excited or if he was up to some mischief of a sort. His curly blonde hair just added to his innocent angelic look. Caleb was so friendly that everyone at school wanted to be friends with him. He was sort of a humble lad, and that too made him likeable.

Once in the garage he looked around for a pair of gloves, but the only ones he saw were his dads. He tried them on but they were way too big for his small hands. So he looked some more and shortly he came upon his batting gloves.

"Wow! At least these will keep me from getting blisters," he thought to himself. So he put them on and ran back to his uncle's house.

Uncle Chip and Caleb work hard all morning getting the area all leveled out. Caleb was beginning to get tired when he felt his shovel hit something with a clinking sound. "What have I found?" he thought. Getting down on his knees he started digging very carefully with his hands. What he saw looked like something made of light green glass. "What kind of treasure have I come upon?" he thought, and he got more excited about the item he had found.

"What's up, Caleb? Have you hit a big rock over there?" asked Uncle Chip. "Do you need me to help you dig it out of the ground?"

"Don't know if I need any help! It's not a rock; it's some kind of green glass whatcha-ma-call-it and it's all caked up with hard dirt clods!" he exclaimed excitedly. "Do you think it could be worth some money? I think it might be a hidden treasure that I've found! Can I keep it?"

Caleb's shovel hit something. But it wasn't a rock only time would tell what treasure he had lucked upon and the adventure that he had just begun.

"It's probably not much of a treasure," laughed Uncle Chip, "It's probably just an old Coca-Cola bottle that got buried in a rubble heap years ago. When your dad and I were kids they used to bottle Cokes in glass instead of putting them in plastic bottles like they do now. I'm afraid that your treasure isn't much of a treasure but if you want to keep it, dig the rest of it up and take it home with you."

"Gee, thanks, Uncle Chip. You know, my Grandpa is always saying, 'one man's junk is another man's treasure,' and you never know when Grandpa is going to be right with one of his sayings."

Caleb wasn't sure what he had but he just knew that it was something very, very special. There was so much dirt around it that the clods appeared to be part of it. So he just began digging around the whole big thing and dragged it over to the basketball goal in his yard, and then went back to finish helping Uncle Chip.

"Caleb, that thing you dug up left a big hole in the area we're trying to level, so how about you doing some filling and packing in that area. The ground has got to be solid and level, okay?" said Uncle Chip.

"Sure thing; I'm doing it right now." Caleb filled in the hole, then took the shovel and smacked the ground good to pack the soil down. Then he added more soil and packed it down until the hole was no longer there. The entire time he worked, his thoughts were racing back to the treasure.

"What if I find out that it's an old jug full of money, wow! I could get a new bike, or I could buy Cissy that new lap-top she needs for school." The more he thought about what he had found, the more excited he got.

"I'm finished!" he cried, "Now, what do you want me to do?"

"How about taking a Coke and sandwich break in the big swing over yonder under that shade tree? Caleb, you have worked so hard I think we both deserve a lunch break, okay? After lunch we'll see if we can get the job finished."

"I'll beatcha there," laughed Caleb. He threw back his head and ran as if he were running for home plate in a championship game. And he beat Uncle Chip, jumped in the swing, leaned back with his hands under his head, with his feet resting on the arms of the swing and said, "Hey, *Unke*, what took you so long?" Then the two of them just burst out laughing and laughing.

"Here, champ, eat up!" said Uncle Chip, "You deserve every bit of this lunch. You have not only come to my rescue today, but son, you have put in a man's worth of work, today. You may only be eleven, but I would choose you to help me any day I need a laborer. Give me a high five, because you are the best worker I've seen!"

After smacking his uncle's hand, Caleb settled down to eat and rest a little before they finished the task.

"Hey, Uncle Chip, this has been fun, but…well…maybe you're giving me more credit for my work than I deserve. Did you ask any of the other boys in the neighborhood to help you?"

"No."

"Do you know Jimmy Sparks over on the next block?" asked Caleb.

"Yes, I think so. Isn't he the one that has the paper route?"

"Yes. And Jimmy is a good worker. He is always stopping on his route to help people. The other day he stopped to help old Mr. Higgins rake up the leaves in his yard. Jimmy would have helped you if you'd asked him to."

"Caleb," said Uncle Chip, "I still think you're great! I appreciate your thoughts about some of the other kids in the neighborhood, and what you have said I'll keep in mind when I have another task that I need help with. There are a lot of good kids out there that like to be helpful to adults. I thank you for reminding me of that fact! Now what do you say about us getting back to work?"

"Whatever you say, boss!" Caleb said laughingly.

The two of them got up and went back to work. All that was left to do was to frame the area with some timbers so Uncle Chip could pour the concrete in and smooth it out, thus providing him with a floor for his new workshop. Caleb wasn't going to help with the cement work, but he did help Uncle Chip put all of the timbers in place and secure them with stakes so as to hold the concrete in place. It had been a real fulfilling day for both Chip and Caleb. They made a good team.

"Bye, Uncle Chip," said Caleb as he was leaving. "Call me if you need any more help this summer, okay?"

"If I need help, Caleb, you will be the first I'll call. But, I'll keep some of those other kids in mind also. Thanks for your help; I couldn't have done it alone." Then good- humouredly Chip called out to Caleb as he was running towards home, "And I hope that thing you dug up turns out to be a treasure and not a dud."

CHAPTER TWO

CALEB'S TREASURE

As soon as Caleb got home he went to work trying to get the glob of dirt off the glass whatever-it-was that he had dug up in Uncle Chip's yard. He felt that he had something special here, but what could it be?

"Boy, this is going to be a hard task. I don't want to break the glass," he reasoned, "just in case it's not a Coca-Cola bottle. Or even if it is a Coca-Cola bottle, maybe a collector might pay a bunch of money for it. Wow! Wouldn't that be great?"

The dirt was more like rock, so Caleb decided to get a chisel and hammer out of his dad's toolbox to see if he could chip it away. Chip, chip, chip, chunk…uh, oh. "I've got to watch what I'm doing" he told himself "hitting the glass is going to make it break or chip." Caleb sat back and looked the situation over for the longest time, when suddenly his concentration was broken by the sound of his Cousin Josh's voice.

"Hey Caleb, whatcha up to, huh?"

"Oh, hi, Josh, I found this thing while I was digging in Uncle Chip's yard this morning," he said excitedly, "and I think I might have found something that is worth some money, maybe. But I'm having a hard time getting it out of this glob of hardened mud. It's almost like stone, so I tried to chisel it off. But, that didn't work too well because the chisel slips and hits the glass part, and I'm afraid it will break or chip the glass, and that will make it worthless."

"I've got an idea," exclaimed Josh. "Let's soak it in a bucket of water. Maybe it will turn those stony clods into mud again and then you can just wash it all off."

"Josh, you're pretty smart!" Caleb laughed, "I would have sat here all day long and not thought about that. Come on, there's a plastic tub in the garage. We can fill it up with water and put this whole chunk in there."

The two boys scrambled off to the garage to find the tub, which just happened to be full of gardening items. Quickly, Caleb and Josh put the items away properly on the shelves in the garage. Each boy grabbed a handle of the now-empty tub, and off they ran to the back yard to fill it with water. They filled the tub with water, and cooled themselves off at the same time - what's a little water squirted back and forth between friends? Then they put the glob of dirt and glass into the tub to let it soak.

Caleb said, "I wonder how long this will take? Do you think we'll need to leave it overnight?"

"Nah! Probably just needs an hour or two," replied Josh. "Why don't we go play 'Donkey' for a while and then come back and try washing it off?"

"Okay, the basketball is on the patio. You go get it and I'm going to go get us a couple of Gatorades."

Caleb and Joshua had been close as brothers since birth. Their mothers were sisters and the boys were born just hours apart. Joshua was the oldest by two hours and a half. He was the smallest at birth, but now he was tall for his age and very lean. Like his mom, he had a full head of auburn hair and freckles across his nose. He was always more shy than Caleb, and quite a worrier. Caleb, on the other hand, was well-suited to his name, which means 'knows no fear'. And most folks who knew the boys agreed that Caleb 'knew no fear' and was the more aggressive of the two. Joshua seemed to enjoy just following Caleb on his adventures.

A couple of hours later the boys were worn out from playing basketball and were ready to sit and whittle on the mud glob. "Josh, this mud is coming off a lot easier than before," Caleb said as he worked. "That was a really good idea you had. Look; I don't know what it is, but it's not a Coke bottle!"

"Caleb, that's pretty strange looking," observed Josh. "It kind of reminds me of something I've seen somewhere before, but it still has too much mud on it to tell what it is."

"Well, don't just stand there and stare, help me get the mud off. Let's take that chisel and use it to help pry it off. Then the water can get down under where some of the dirt is still dry. I just know we got ourselves something special here. Something real special, you just wait and see, yes siree-bob-a-link-o!"

An hour and a half later the boys finally removed all of the mud to reveal a long green glass cylinder about seventeen inches long with a three inch circumference in the middle, with each end measuring three inches long by one-and-half inches in circumference, and a rusty lid attached to one of the smaller ends.

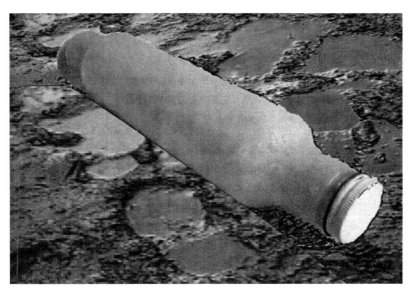

"What kind of a thing-a-ma-jig do you think we've unearthed here?" said Caleb very quizzically. He was really beginning to wonder if he had any sort of a real treasure. It definitely wasn't looking like what he was hoping for.

"Hey, I've seen another one just like it; I know what it is!" exclaimed Josh.

"Well, tell me quick, don't keep me in suspense," exclaimed Caleb, "What is this thing?"

"Well, Granny Alfred has one just like that, but hers is made of white glass and she uses it to roll out pie dough. You know, like a rolling pin, but she puts cold water in it first and then she rolls the dough," said Josh.

"You got to be kidding! All this work for a stupid old rolling pin, and now what can we do with it?" Just then something caught Caleb's eye. "Look, there's something inside. Looks like a message in a bottle. Do you suppose someone hid this on purpose?"

"Well, I don't know, and you won't know either if you don't open it up! Let's read what it says!" said Josh. "I'm as excited as you are, but let's find out what we really have. It could be a grocery list, you know," he added.

"Okay, hang on a minute, this lid is not only rusty-it's stuck!"

"Well, unstuck it!"

Caleb fell over in laughter. "Josh, you are so funny. You want me to 'unstuck it,' huh? Well, get me something to 'unstuck it' with. And I'll promise to let you read it, too."

Josh went to the garage, found a pair of channel-locks and brought them out to Caleb. "These I know will have a wide enough mouth on them to get hold of that lid," he said. Caleb gripped the lid with the channel-locks and Josh got hold of the container. "Josh," said Caleb, "you turn the container to the right and I'll pull with the wrench to the left. The lid's on there tight so push with all of your might."

The boys tore the rusty metal cap off the end of the bottle and tossed it aside. Then they removed some well-preserved pieces of paper: a letter addressed to "Whomever Finds These Notes"; a page filled with riddles and clues; a map; and a floor plan of a house.

"What have we found?" breathed Caleb. "I think we are about to have ourselves an adventure!"

"Caleb, I think we better give this stuff to your parents or your uncle," Josh said with fear and trembling. "Do you realize we might be getting ourselves into something that is way too big for us boys to handle?"

"Josh, don't wimp out on me now! We don't need to give these to anyone. Besides, Uncle Chip said I could have what I found. And the letter is addressed to "Whomever Finds These Notes", and that's us. Don't you agree?"

"Okay! But I have a feeling something creepy is going to happen, and I'm going to be sorry for going along with you on this so-called adventure."

"What's a cousin for, huh? Trust me, if it looks dangerous I'll call my Dad. But first, let's see what this is all about. Let's start by reading the letter and then we'll inch our way along after that, and I promise if the going gets too tough, I'll call in the big guy--" he said as he puffed out his chest and pumped up his arms and in a strong voice cried "--DAD! And you know he'll come to the rescue right away!"

With his shoulders slumping, hanging his head, and giving in as he always seemed to do, Josh said in a defeated tone, "Oh, all right. But let's not take too big a chance before calling in the back-up, okay?"

"Good," smiled Caleb. "You clean up the tub and put it back in the garage and meet me in my bedroom in fifteen minutes. I'll make us some sandwiches and get some chips and drinks. After all, we need food to energize our thinking process."

CHAPTER THREE
MYSTERIOUS CONTENTS

Within twenty minutes the two boys were scrunched down in beanbag chairs in Caleb's room, nibbling on refreshments and trying to sort out the contents of the container that they had just opened up.

"Okay, Josh, let's get organized." Caleb said with the tone of a business professional. "I think we should read this letter and find out what this is all about. Surely the letter will give us a clue as to what all of these other things are for or what we're supposed to do with them."

"All right, Caleb, why don't you read the letter out loud? I'll try to listen for clues and write them down on my notepad," replied Josh.

Caleb began slowly reading aloud the contents of the letter addressed to "Whomever Finds These Notes".

I, Jacob Timberlake, being of sound mind at the time of this writing, have decided that my family is undeserving of my true inheritance and therefore I have hidden my personal treasures from them. I now instruct the finder of this letter to follow my directions, and clues, and then solve the riddles that will lead you to find what I have left behind in this world and have hidden from my family.

First, you will need to go to my estate which is called "The Timbers." I have placed with these contents a map showing how to get from where I have hidden these items to where my estate is located on Cottonwood Grove Road. I do this fearing that the names of streets and places may have changed by the time these contents are found. Once you have arrived at the estate, you will need to find your way around-that is, presuming that the estate still remains standing. To help you find your way around once you are inside the house, I have included a floor plan. This will help you to quickly locate the areas I am sending you to.

Be very careful when following these directions. Read the clues, then read and solve the riddles. Each clue and riddle will, in some instances, lead you to an item you will need to solve the next clue, so be sure to solve them in the order that they appear.

Keep this letter in a safe place, so if any of my family members should try to stop you from claiming what they think should belong to them, you will have my signed and notarized letter giving to you all that you find.

Good luck on your adventure. I will be tucked away in my grave laughing at all that will be happening.

Respectfully yours,

Jacob Timberlake

At the end of the letter was a separate note, which read,

I hereby certify that the letter to which my seal has been affixed is the originally written letter of Jacob Timberlake, who being of sound mind, does on this day turns over his entire worldly goods to the finder of this letter. Witness my hand and the seal of my notary as licensed to me by the Coffee County Court of Tennessee this 16th day of September 1959.

Melissa R. Grimes, Notary

"Golly, this sounds like it's a for real document," Joshua whispered. "We had better find someplace safe to keep this letter; else we might find ourselves in a heap of trouble if we find Mr. Timberlake's personal treasures and his family decides to have us arrested or something."

"I know just the place to put this letter." Caleb went scurrying into the other part of the house and came back with an envelope. "We'll put the letter in this envelope and tape the envelope shut. Then let's write our names over the seal – that way we can tell if anyone should happen to tamper with this at all."

"Okay, but where are you going to keep it after we do that?" asked Josh.

"Just go ahead and put your name across the flap and then I'll show ya."

"There now," said Josh, "my name is on this end and yours is on the other. So show me where you are going to put it."

Caleb got a chair, went over to the closet and opened the door. He placed the chair just inside the closet.

"Caleb, you can't just lay it on the shelf. Your mom or sisters will be sure to find it," said Joshua with a frown. "You need a better place than that!"

"Hang on a minute, wouldja!" said Caleb as he climbed up on the chair and then turned around to face the door opening. Reaching up above the door facing, he took the envelope, and forced its edge between the wall and the door facing. After successfully stuffing it in place, he climbed down and gleefully said, "No one will ever think of looking for something stuck up there on the door facing."

"Gosh, you're always coming up with such clever ideas. Now what are we going to do about the rest of this stuff?" asked Josh.

Caleb picked up the map and said, "Let's see if we can figure out how far away it is from here to this place called 'The Timbers.'" He spread the map out on the floor and both boys looked it over, trying to get their bearings on just where the map was going to lead them.

"Uh-huh," said Caleb as he pointed to the map. "That road there is just across the road from our house, Josh. Look-that's the road that goes out to the college, and you know what? I think I know exactly where 'The Timbers' is," he said with excitement in his voice. "Come on, get your bike-we're going over there right now!"

"Whoa, hang on a minute, Caleb," cautioned Josh, "it could be a long ways out there and I'm not sure that I want in on this adventure of yours. It still sounds a little too scary for me. And what makes you think anyone would let you into the house when you get there? I know that **you're** not scared of anything, but I am. I get scared of plundering around in someone else's business, and I'm also afraid of the whipping my dad will give me if I mess up. So maybe I'll just pedal on home and let you have this adventure on your own!"

"Josh, you're this biggest scaredy cat I've ever known. You make me ashamed to call you my cousin," Caleb said with his head hung down. Then he gave the floor a big old stomp. "All I said was we should get on our bikes and take a ride out that way and see if we can find 'The Timbers'- I didn't say anything about trying to go into the house or do anything at all except find where the place is. And you, my cuz, want to wimp out!"

"I'm not wimping out!" retorted Josh. "I'm just cautious. If you promise to ride out that way and look for the place and then come right back, I'll go with you. But, you have to promise that's all were going to do, okay?"

"Okay! I just want to know if 'The Timbers' is still there and if we can find it using this map. The map is dated 'September, 1959' and that was a long, long time ago. Hey, the place could have been torn down and a new house built on the land, so come on and let's go take a peek."

"Let's get the bikes and go then. I need to be back before mom calls to check on me," replied Josh. "I told her I was only going to play over here for a couple of hours, and she'll be home from work in another hour. I sure don't want her worrying about me."

"I know what we'll do," said Caleb. "I'll leave a note for my mom by the phone. I'll tell her that we've gone for a bike ride and if your mom calls, she should tell her we'll be home in time for supper.

And I'll ask her to see if you can spend the night with us, Okay?" Caleb talked faster and faster with each sentence he spoke. "My sisters, Cissy and Macula, are gone and Mom and Dad need some time to themselves, so since tomorrow is Saturday we can work some more on this little adventure, huh! That is, if you want to spend the night and do that tomorrow! What do you say, cuz?"

"I say that I think I'm going to be sorry for giving in to you, but yeah-tell your mom to ask my mom if I can spend the night and stay here tomorrow, too."

CHAPTER FOUR

THE TIMBERS

"Over this way, Josh," Caleb shouted, "this is the old road that goes out to the college. Come on and catch up with me."

"I'm pedaling as fast I can! Give me a break, will ya? You said we were just going to follow the map to the location, you didn't tell me we were racing to get there."

Pedaling ahead, Caleb said, "Well, I think that Cottonwood Grove Road is that gravel road that leads off to the right just after you cross the bridge over the Forked Deer Branch. If that is the road, then we're in for a really bumpy ride. I don't think any cars have been up that road in a long time."

"Hey, Caleb, slow down will ya!" Joshua had sweat pouring down his face and he was really tuckered out. Gasping for air, he reminded Caleb of how hot and sultry the air was, and suggested that they both take a rest and get a drink of water.

"I'll make you a deal! Keep pedaling 'til we get to the Forked Deer and we'll not only stop for a drink, we'll go wading in the water and get good and cooled off before we turn off on the Cottonwood Grove Road," suggested Caleb.

"Just for that, I'll race you to the bridge!" exclaimed Joshua.

Those two boys got to the bridge, parked the bikes, rolled up their pant legs, kicked off their shoes and socks and were up to their knees in the water before you could say 'Jumpin' Jack Sprat'. They shouted, giggled and splashed water on each other. Josh took a big handful of water and dumped it right over Caleb's head, then laughingly said, "Now that's what I call a wet head!" Later, Caleb began skipping rocks down the stream, and the boys got into a contest to see whose rock could skip the farthest as well as the most times.

Finally they tired of the water play and decided to get on with looking for 'The Timbers'. Of course they had to take time to put their shoes and socks back on. Socks and shoes were dry but the boys had managed to get everything else soaking wet.

"We better be dry by the time we get home," Caleb exclaimed, "or mom might be a little put out with us."

"I don't think you have to worry about that. As hot as it is, we should be bone dry in no time at all!" replied his cousin.

"If you're ready," Caleb said, "we'll get to biking down the road to the Cottonwood Gove turn-off. It shouldn't be much farther if it's the road I think it is."

As they pedaled around the bend from the bridge, they spotted a gravel road running off to the right. They slowed their bikes down and began looking around the area and up the gravel road.

"Caleb," said Josh, "I don't see any markers to indicate the name of the road. It might just lead up into the woods or up to some farmer's pasture."

"No, look at all of that brush across the road up there. I don't think that anyone ever uses this road. I think we ought to venture up the road and see if we see any houses. If it's a pasture or a dead end, we'll just come back and go on down the road a little farther. But, well…well, I'm pretty sure this is Cottonwood Grove Road, sign or no sign."

The boys got off of their bikes and pushed them up the road, which was gravel and full of ruts and in pretty rough condition. Since the bikes were street bikes, the terrain was too difficult for them to be ridden. Finally Caleb suggested that they just leave the bikes and continue up the road on foot.

About twenty minutes later the two of them spotted a large fence looming up before them. "I think this must be 'The Timbers'!" Caleb said confidently. But it was not exactly what they had expected a grand estate to look like. Bushes and weeds were grown up all around the place. A huge iron and brick fence encompassed the estate; each iron prong loomed high above them and was topped with an iron arrowhead, making the fence look like a long string of huge spears. An enormous gate greeted them with the words, 'The Timbers' scrolled in iron hanging high above the gate. "This is definitely the place!" shouted Caleb. "Let's open the gate and take a peek inside."

"You have to be kidding!" exclaimed Josh. "That gate was put there to keep people out, and you want to barge right on in! I think its time for us to high-tail it back to home before it gets dark."

"Yeah, you're right," said Caleb. "But it won't hurt just to open the gate; we don't have to go in just yet. We can wait until tomorrow to do that."

Reluctantly Josh agreed to help Caleb open the gate. Both boys tried very hard to push it open, but it wouldn't budge.

"This gate must be rusted shut! Look at how the rust is built up around the hinges," Caleb said.

"Great!" shouted Josh with relief, "that means we can't get in if we wanted to, so let's get out of here!"

"You're right for now, but our grandpa taught me how to get rusted things undone. So hang on to your hat, we're coming back tomorrow with all of the right stuff to get us through the gates and on to the house." Wheeling around, Caleb tracked off in the direction of the bikes. Then he shouted back to Josh who was just standing there scratching his chin and looking at the gate, "Are you coming with me, or do I have to go home alone?"

"I'm coming," Josh said in a muffled tone, "yeah, I'm right behind you. But I don't have a clue as to what you plan to do with that gate. Nope, I haven't a clue."

Back-tracking down, the gravel road, they located their bikes propped against the tree where they'd left them and they started pushing the bikes down to the main road.

"Boy, we'll have to ride fast or it's going to get dark before we can get back to the house," said Caleb. "I want to have time to put some things together for our trip back here tomorrow. Least ways I hope your mom is going to let you spend the night so we can come back here together."

The boys got home just in time, as Caleb's mom was about to start looking for them.

"Where have you youngsters been?" she asked. "Don't you know its getting too dark to ride your bikes?"

"Yes, ma'am, that's why we're coming in. Did you see my note?" asked Caleb.

"Yes, Caleb, thank you for leaving it," said his mother. "And Josh, I've talked with your mom, and she said that since your sister is working tomorrow, it would be all right for you to spend the night and all day tomorrow with us. Besides, your uncle George and I are planning a cookout for tomorrow evening and we have invited your family, so everything will work out just fine. Now, you boys get washed up for supper."

With a high-five to each other, the two boys gleefully ran into the house and got themselves ready for supper.

CHAPTER FIVE

THE NEXT MORNING

Caleb woke up real early in the morning and quickly got dressed. He was filled with excitement and wanted to get started right away. He tried to get Josh to wake up. "Hey, Josh you're sleeping the day away! Get up, boy, and let's get biking down the road."

"Yawn…what time is it?" asked a very sleepy Josh.

"It's 6:00 a.m. and we have a lot to do today!"

"6:00 a.m.? No intelligent person gets up before 8:00 am on a Saturday morning. Caleb, you've got to be kidding me. I want to sleep for a couple more hours."

"You sleep. I'm going to get everything that we will need packed up." Caleb said as he prepared to organize everything. He was the leader and he would make sure they had proper equipment for their quest.

"But when I come back" he told Josh, "you better be ready to roll out of that bed, or else I'll pour ice water on you. Do you understand?"

"Yeah, now leave me alone, will ya?"

Caleb ran out to the garage and began searching for anything that might be helpful.

"Grandpa has always said, 'If anything is stuck and it's metal, get out the WD-40 and you'll have it freed up in a short time,'" Caleb remembered. So the first thing he put into his backpack was a large can of WD-40. Then he added some clothesline rope, a couple of shop towels, a hammer, a small flip-out camping saw, one regular flashlight and one clip-on lamp, a camping hatchet, and his trusty Swiss Army knife.

"Whew! I'm glad that I was able to fit all of that into my backpack," he thought to himself. "Now I'm going to have to put the water, Gatorade, chips, cookies, and sandwiches all into Josh's backpack. Then we'll be ready to go!"

Returning to the house, Caleb headed for the kitchen, where his mom was making breakfast. In a very polite tone of voice he asked, "Hey, Mom, would you fix some sandwiches for Josh and me? We want to put them in our backpacks with some chips, cookies, and drinks."

"And why do you need that much food so early in the morning and before you've even had your breakfast?" she replied.

"Josh is getting up and we are going to eat our breakfast. But then we've made plans to ride our bikes down by the Forked Deer and we're going to be playing there where it's cool. Gosh, we thought you and dad might like a day to spend alone and Josh and I will entertain each other! Doesn't that sound like a good plan?"

Laughingly she admitted that their plan sounded good. Besides, she had a lot of shopping to do to get ready for the cookout that night.

"I'll fix your lunches," she agreed. "You just get Josh and come to breakfast. Oh, by the way, I think you should clean up your room before you go biking any place. Am I understood on that ruling?" she said sternly.

"Yes, ma'am, I'll get started right away!" With those words, Caleb rushed down the hall to his room where he once again urged Josh to get up.

"Josh, I'm giving you to the count of three and then I'm going to get a pitcher of ice water!" said Caleb threateningly.

"Okay, okay!" said a sleepy Josh as he yawned, stretched and got out of bed. "I'm headed for the bathroom; just give me a minute to get my eyes unglued."

"While you're sprucing up, I'm going to pick up the mess in my room and make the bed. Mom just about has breakfast ready, and I want to get going as soon as we finish eating."

After breakfast, the boys said thanks and good-bye to Caleb's parents and off they scurried on their bikes. This time they knew exactly where they were going and they sped off quickly in that direction. With a whoop and a shout Caleb said, "With this early start we have the whole day to explore Mr. Timberlake's place!"

With a quivering voice, Josh said, "I just pray that there are no wild dogs, ghosts, or other things to get in our way. All I want to do is find these things and get out of there! I hope you remembered to bring everything so we can make just one trip to this place. It was creepy looking, and I don't want to be caught there after dark!"

"Oh, Josh," Caleb shouted, "quit complaining and let's have a good time. What could happen to us in an old empty house, anyway?"

"Just because your name means 'no fear'," Josh challenged, "doesn't mean that the rest of us have no fear. And even if you fear nothing, well," he said with a big gulp, "things can still happen to you, so let's be cautious! Okay?"

"You win! I'll be as cautious as can be. And I'm doing it just for you, cuz."

CHAPTER SIX

AT THE TIMBERS

Arriving at The Timbers, Caleb opened up his backpack and proceeded to work on getting through the large gate.

"Here, I'm taking our grandpa's advice and we're going to spray these hinges with some WD-40," he said to Josh. "That should break loose all the rust that's holding the gate closed."

"Great!" sighed Josh as he eyed the gate from top to bottom. "But how do you plan on reaching that hinge at the top of the gate?"

"With your help, anything is possible!" said Caleb with a twinkle in his eye.

"Oh, yeah?" questioned Josh. "And just how am I going to help? I don't have a ladder or a pair of stilts with me."

"Gimme a minute, will you, to finish this hinge." In a few minutes, Caleb reached in his backpack and pulled out the clothesline. He made a lasso in one end of the rope.

"Grandpa taught me, just like he taught Dad, how to make this lasso. Now all I have to do is throw it over one of those fence rods sticking up there. Then, my friend, you can help me shinny up the rope so I can reach that top hinge to spray some WD-40 there also."

Caleb made about ten attempts to lasso the fence rod before he was successful. Then while Josh held the rope taut, he shinnied up the rope and was able to cover the hinge with the lubricant.

"Now we just need to give it a little time to work. While we are waiting, how about helping to get this rope back. We may need it again later."

The two of them struggled for a time, trying to loosen the lasso and jerk the rope from the top of the fence rod. Finally in despair, Caleb said, "We're getting nowhere, so how's about you steadying my bike and I'll stand on the handlebars and reach up as high as I can and just cut the rope with my knife."

"I don't feel too good about that," said Josh, "what if you fall off and get hurt? You know it's a long way back to the house from here, especially if your leg gets broke or something else!"

"Josh, I wish you would quit being so negative about everything. We might need this rope and I want to save as much of it as I can. Now get over here *puh-lease* and hold this bike for me."

Reluctantly and worriedly, Josh held the bicycle steady while Caleb cut the rope down and put it into his backpack. About fifteen minutes later the boys pushed hard against the gate. It creaked and moaned a lot, but finally gave way enough where the two of them could skedaddle inside.

Now they met an even bigger challenge, for the road leading from the gate to the house was thick with weeds, spider webs, underbrush, broken tree limbs, and all kinds of debris.

"Here," commanded Caleb, "you take the hatchet and I'll take the saw and we'll chop our way through to the house." After looking around for a moment or two to decide where the path of least resistance was, they decided to try and stay on the drive going straight to the house. They found it easy to chop a path through the debris, except for one small tree that blocked the path; they just climbed over the trunk where it lay and proceeded chopping. It was fifteen or twenty minutes before they reached the house.

There it stood looming above them. It was three stories high, and its windows were dirty. Some were broken. In places, the molding was broken and hanging off. Ornate ironwork trimmed the main entrance, the top and rails of the porch, and the edges of the roof. On the second story was a large balcony with its iron railing dangling precariously at the right end of the balcony. On the third story were the remnants of two smaller balconies. The bricks on the lower half were worn but intact, while most of the woodwork was rotten or falling off. Spider webs could be seen everywhere. The main porch looked unsafe to walk on and the double doors were made of heavy timber. There were no windows in, or beside the door, just a big, discolored, brass door knocker that was hanging precariously by one screw. The doors looked foreboding, and like something out of a monster movie. All in all, the house was neglected and in bad shape, and a little scary to look at.

"Let's look at the floor plan," said Caleb, "'cause we need to know where we're going to start. Guess I better get the directions, clues and riddles out and read them, too. We need to be courageous as we follow these clues."

"Yeah, yeah,' so let's get on with it before I lose my courage and go home!" said Josh nervously.

"Look here," said Caleb excitedly, as he pointed to the paper in his hand, "the starting place is in bold print. It says, 'Go to the closet under the grand staircase.' And looking at these floor plans," he said hesitantly, "it looks like the grand staircase is going to be directly behind that scary-looking door." After studying the porch he added, "We may as well get started. Huh, let's read over all of these clues first and get a feel for where we're going once we get inside the house. Then we can go from there; does that sound like a good plan to you?"

The Timbers
Home of Jacob Timberlake

First Floor

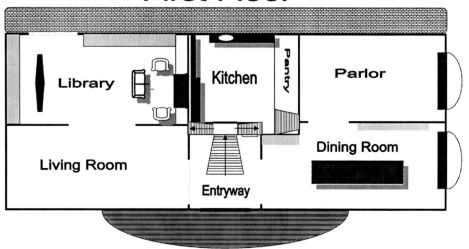

Basement - Recreation Room

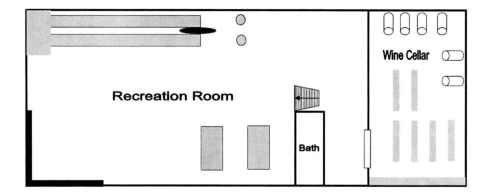

Second Floor

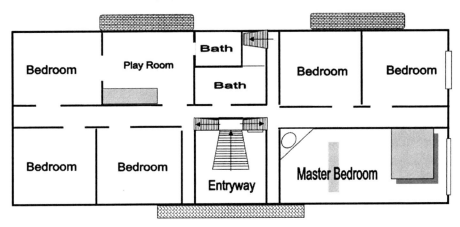

Third Floor

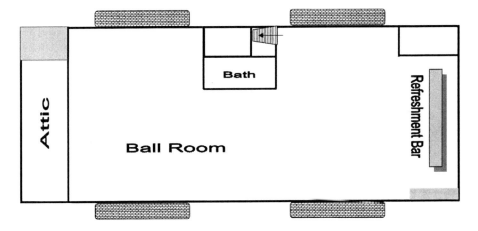

"Right now the best plan in my opinion is to high-tail it out of here before something bad happens to us. This whole place looks eerie and unsafe! I just have bad vibes about the whole thing, and I don't know why I let you talk me into doin' this," said Josh anxiously.

"Shucks, Josh, you have no adventure in your bones at all," teased Caleb.

"I'm proud of my bones just like they are, and I don't need any adventure in them! And I don't want any of them to get broken way out here. Our families don't even know where we are," Josh complained. "What if something were to happen, what if we were to get trapped inside or hurt? No one would know where to look for us, now would they? That alone scares me, and should scare you too."

"Lay off the negatives," Caleb retorted, "and let's see what positive things we have going for us. We won't get hurt, 'cause we'll be careful. It's an old house and we can see the condition it's in, so we'll just take it slow and easy and watch where we're going. Now let me read these instructions to ya."

WHOMEVER FINDS THESE NOTES

Enclosed are the directions for finding my most precious belongings. The floor plans will help you to locate the area. Each place where I have hidden an item, you will need to collect that item. I have written a riddle that you MUST solve in order to gain access to the hidden item. You will need every one of these items before the hunt is over and you can obtain access into the hideaway, where my treasures lies.

Main Floor of 'The Timbers'

1. Go to the closet under the grand staircase.

    First clue: Hobis knobis in kamisas, in the knobis find the keysus.

2. Go to the grand dining room.

    Second clue: With light shining above, I'm alone in the dark.

    I'm stuck in the lid that someone sits upon.

    When you find me here, remember, I've an identical twin that is near.

2. Go to the parlor.

    Third clue: Have you found my twin?

    If so remember parlor décor is always ornate. Ornate I may seem to be, but unattached I may serve thee.

4. Go to the library.

    Fourth clue: In the library are many books, so many items can be found. Flames above the hearth protect that what doth lurk in the ground.

    Fifth clue: Bookcases are tricky and seem so tall; one might conceal something quite small. Ivanhoe would know what to do. Behind him, Joan of Arc and Robin of Loxley, you might find that for which you're looking.

5. Go to the second floor.

   Sixth clue: Many porches and rooms to adore, secret panels or a hidden door, the playroom closet holds a surprise, many items I did hide. Find ten on that floor, then up to the third floor for some more.

6. Go to the third floor.

   Seventh clue: Mirror, mirror on the wall, what behind me must I see to gain access and relieve my stress.

   The Western sun shines a ray of light, open a door and behold the sight. If you can't figure this one out, you may have to sit and pout.

   Eighth clue: Somewhere you'll find my moniker; take it with you, for surely there's a proper place to affix such a thing.

7. Go to the basement.

   Ninth clue: Under the green between the pockets, lies a prize if you can unlock it.

   Tenth clue: Ten pins and alleys, cats and feathers, what you need is in plain sight between where two balls might roll into sight.

   Eleventh clue: Now you must go through the gate for that is where you'll find your fate. I have helped you all I can; now you solve the rest of the plan. For if you solve this mystery, all the possessions I value are yours to keep.

When Caleb had finished reading all of the clues aloud, Josh said, "Caleb, that sounds like a lot of work. How in the world are we going to find the answers to all of those riddles? I'm beginning to think this Timberlake fellow is - or was crazy. I'm all for dropping this whole thing right now and getting out of here!"

Caleb looked at Josh with surprise. "Come on, Josh!" he said. "We've come this far, so let's just see if we can solve a couple of the first riddles. If we can, then we know we can go on and find the treasure. I promise if we can't solve some of the first clues, we'll go home and I'll just give all of the stuff to my dad. Okay?"

"Why didn't you give it to your dad in the first place?" asked Josh.

"'Cause the summer is about over, and I wanted to say that I had some kind of an adventure. All I've done this summer is play baseball and hang around the house with my sisters. Now I have a chance for a bit of a challenge, and you should be a little excited about all of this, too."

"Well…well, maybe," Josh admitted. "Shucks, we're here, so let's get on with it! Where should we start?"

"I suggest we carefully get up on that porch and walk over to the door to see if it's unlocked."

The boys gathered up their equipment and slowly ascended the broken-down steps leading up to the porch. Testing each step they made, lest they fall through some rotted floor boards, they crept over to the door. It looked big from where they were on the ground, but when they stood beside it, they noticed just how enormous it really was. Caleb tried the latch, only to find it didn't work.

"Guess we'll have to find some other way to get into this house," he said as he scratched his head in puzzlement. "I just figured with everything else falling apart, this door would be falling apart, too. Guess I'm wrong - it's still big and strong. Let's try opening one of these windows."

Though the boys tried, they couldn't open any of the windows on the front of the house. So they went back to hacking at the underbrush around the house so that they could reach the back of the house. There they found a porch in much disrepair that ran the full length of the house. Once again testing their every step, they cautiously walked the length of the porch, stopping only to try each window. Coming upon a set of locked French doors, Caleb said with confidence, "I can get us in through these doors!"

"Oh, yeah!" asked Josh. "Whatcha goin' to do--break the glass panes?"

"No, I'm going to use my knife! I learned a little trick about these kinds of doors from watching a burglar on a TV show. All I have to do is stick my knife right here between the doors and press against this here toggle connection and…and…and it's a little harder than I thought!" he said, in exasperation.

"That's whatcha get for believing every thing you see on TV," Josh said wryly.

"Ah, just give me a minute or two." Caleb said as he continued to struggle with the door latch. After innumerable tries, he succeeded in opening the door. "Voila- it works!"

"Well, let's walk carefully. I don't want any surprises - such as a hole to fall into."

The boys cautiously stepped in and gave their eyes a little time to adjust to the dimmer light inside.

"Gosh, Josh," exclaimed Caleb. "Look at all of those books! He must have been rich enough to own his own library. And his family left without taking the books with 'em. That's the craziest thing. You'd think that they would at lest give those books to the library in town."

They had found themselves in a very large room with bookshelves lining all of the walls. The shelves ran all the way up to the ceiling, and the ceilings were extremely high. It was high enough up to have a walkway about midway up the wall, with a spiral staircase in the corner. A long study table was at the west end of the room and a large fireplace was at the east end. A huge old desk sat just six feet in front of the shelves on the north wall. They also found an overstuffed leather sofa and two chairs facing the fireplace on the south wall. None of the furnishings was in very good condition and everything smelled musty and dank. The boys were amazed at the size and condition of this room and they continued looking about the library.

Feeling hungry from all the energy that they used just to reach this one room in the house, Joshua suggested that they sit a spell and eat some of the food Caleb's mom had fixed for them. They carefully checked out the sofa to see whether it was sturdy enough for them to sit on. It was covered with a thick layer of dust and the leather was hard, but it supported their weight just fine, so they broke out their lunch and took a much-needed rest.

CHAPTER SEVEN
BEGINNING TO SOLVE THE RIDDLES

"Hey, Caleb," asked Josh. "Didn't some of those riddles have to do with this room?"

"Yes," Caleb admitted, "but I think we're supposed to go to all of these places in a particular order. And it says we should start with the grand staircase closet."

"Okay," said Josh, "let's get looking for that closet."

The boys were still unsure about the flooring in the old house, but it appeared to be in better condition than the porches were. To be on the safe side, they tested every step they took.

Leaving the library, they entered a big empty room. On the south wall was a large window, with torn, rotting curtains. A musty, rag-tag carpet lay on the floor in the middle of the room. On all four sides there was about three feet of wood flooring between the carpet and the wall. Nothing else was in that room.

Walking through the archway on the east side of the room, they found themselves at the foot of the grand staircase. The staircase was very wide at the bottom and got narrower as it approached a landing half-way to the second floor. Then the stairs split and half went to the left while the other half went to the right. Wide, winding banisters were attached to each side. It was the kind of staircase that invited children to slide down its banisters, but after a closer inspection, the boys decided it would be better not to attempt such a thing now.

"Caleb, where do you think the closet is?" asked Josh as he peered around.

"Most staircase closets are underneath the steps," answered his cousin. "My Dad's mom had her closet made into an extra bathroom. Boy, did that come in handy when we went to visit her. With her and grandpa, then me, mom, dad and two sisters, well, we needed lots of bathrooms!" he laughed.

"Let's look around on the other side," encouraged Caleb. The boys walked around to the right side of the staircase and noticed a door straight ahead of them. "Let's see where that door goes," said the ever-curious Caleb.

"Just the kitchen," reported Josh as he peered into the room. "But look," he pointed out, "there's a door in the side of the staircase. Caleb, I bet this is the one we're looking for." He opened the door to verify that it was, indeed, the closet and then asked, "So what's the riddle?"

Caleb got the papers out and looked for the first clue. Then he read, "Hobis knobis in kamisas, in the knobis find the keysus."

Joshua reopened the door and felt around in the dark, trying his best to find a light switch, but had no success.

"If you could find it, do you think it would work?" chided Caleb. He reached into his backpack and took out the hand- held flashlight for Joshua and the clip-on light which he attached to his cap. Then they took a second look in the closet, but all they found was an old deteriorated broom, a rotted mop, and lots of dirt and darkness. "It's empty," they said at the same time, and laughed.

"Now what?" asked Josh.

"Just start feeling around," said Caleb, "Maybe there's a secret door."

After feeling around for some time, they concluded that there was no secret door. "Okay, I give up!" said Josh. "Do those crazy words make any sense to you?"

Caleb thought, "No. But it would help if I knew what we were looking for! Hobis knobis in kamisas. Hmmm, what's a Hobis?"

"Hey, maybe it's one of those poem things where the first letter of each word spells out something!"

"Great idea, Josh, but H-K-I-K-I-T-K-F-T-K doesn't spell anything," Caleb said with a sigh. After studying the words for some time, he suddenly announced, "I got an idea! Let's underline what appears to be known words and see if that gives us a clue!"

"I don't have anything to write with do you?" asked Josh.

"Oh, yeah, I packed everything I could think of in this backpack!" Caleb said happily and rummaged through his stuff until he came up with a pen.

"Now then, give me a little help here," he said to Josh as he took the paper over to a window where the light was a lot better.

Josh read the clue, and then said, "Well, the first word is Hobis! I know what a Hobbit is, but not a Hobis."

"Hey, look at the next word!" said Caleb. "Knobis, if you underline just the knob and then the is it says, 'knob is'!"

"Well, you can do the same thing to the first word and it says, 'hob is'. But the hob and knob is what?"

"Knob is a **knob**-like a door knob! Hey-let's check this here closet door knob and see if it comes off," Caleb said as he tugged hard at the door knob. "My goodness gracious, it won't budge an inch. It's a good thing that I brought a few tools with me. Here, you hold the door and I'll get a screwdriver and see if we can take the thing apart."

"Boy, Caleb, you think of everything!" marveled Josh.

"It's so far back to home that I wanted to make sure that we had everything we needed without having to make a trip back to the house," Caleb explained.

Josh agreed, "It's a good thing that you brought those tools."

After locating the screwdriver in his backpack, Caleb began loosening the screws that held the door knob in place. It was pretty hard to do since some of the screws were rusty.

"I may have to use some WD-40 on these screws," Caleb grunted as he put all of his efforts into undoing the screws, "'cause that's the only thing I know of that will unbind rust on screws."

So saying, he brought out the WD-40 and sprayed the screws liberally. Then he took the screwdriver and with all of the strength that he could muster up, "Vivola, it's loose!" he said happily. "Now let's see what's so special about this knob."

"All you have is a square rod and two knobs. Nothin' special 'bout that!" observed Josh.

"Wait a minute," Caleb said thoughtfully, and he began to shake the two knobs. One of them made a rattling noise. "Hey," he said, "there's something in this knob. But how am I going to get it out?"

"You know what?" said Josh. "Those knobs are different than the ones in our house. Look-the knob has a seam. It's made up of two halves so all you need to do is cut it open on the seam. Did ya bring some scissors with ya?"

"No!" moaned Caleb.

"What shall we do now?" questioned Josh.

"If you can hold the knob still I think I can use the screwdriver and a hammer to pry it open," said Caleb.

"How do you plan to do that? I'm not going to put my hand down there for you to smash it with a slip of the hammer. No sirree, Bob!"

"Look, Josh, all I have to do is fasten the knob back on the rod. Then you can hold the rod and keep the knob from rolling while I work on it." Caleb quickly reattached the knob to the rod and handed it to Joshua. Then both boys returned to the staircase where Joshua placed the knob on one of the steps and held it tightly while Caleb worked feverishly on the knob with the hammer and screwdriver. After a good fifteen minutes of banging around, the two pieces split and out on the step fell a key.

With growing excitement, Josh said, "Look, Caleb, it's a key! But what are we supposed to use the key to unlock?"

"I don't know, there's no clue here. Let's put it in the pocket of my bag and go looking for some of these other items. Maybe we will run across a lock that needs unlocking."

A puzzled Josh inquired, "Where shall we go next?"

"The next item is supposed to be in that room. So let's find the dining room." Caleb and Josh started looking around. "Well, I don't think it was the room we just came through so let's try the room to the left of the front door," suggested Caleb.

As they entered the room, Josh exclaimed, "Wow! This is it - look at the size of that table! Why would someone go off and leave such a big table behind?"

"Josh, just think-how many tables that size could you get in a normal-size home? You need a mansion for something that big. I don't even think it would fit into a moving van!"

"You're probably right," admitted Josh, "so what's the clue for this room?"

Caleb read the clue again. *"With light shining above, I'm alone in the dark. I'm stuck in the lid that someone sits upon. When you find me here, remember, I've an identical twin that is near.*

Now, how in the world can you be in the dark if light is shining above?" Caleb wondered.

"Well," exclaimed Josh, "there's light coming through that big window over here and again through that window at the end of the room and also, some light is coming through the door that leads to another room. I don't see any dark spots!"

"It says it is stuck in the lid. Do you see anything around here with a lid on it?"

Both boys wandered about the room, looking high and low for anything that looked like a lid or like it might have a lid.

"I can't see anything in here but that huge table, those two dish cabinets, and a window bench. That's all," Josh said disgustedly.

"Hey, I think I've got it." Caleb said excitedly. "Yeap, that has to be it! Stuck in a lid someone sits upon…my Aunt Frances had a window bench in her house and the lid opened up and a storage box was inside of it. Boy, we use to have fun playing hide-n-seek in her house! There would always be a bunch of us playin' and sure as I'm standin' here, one of us would end up hidin' in the window bench."

The two ran over to the bench and slowly opened it up. It was full of cobwebs, old, smelly, bug-infested newspapers, a couple of well-used candles, and a pillow with its stuffing falling out.

"Well, Caleb, that turned out to be a lost cause. I don't see another key or anything else worth having. Do you?" asked Josh.

"Wait!" Caleb said with determination, "we didn't finish the clue...it...it...a...it says...'I'm stuck in the lid.'" Excitedly Caleb explained, "It didn't say anything about being in the bench."

The boys began to examine the lid more closely. "Look!" exclaimed Caleb. "See that funny shaped cut out in the lid?"

"Yeah, you're right! Here, I'll hold the lid and you see if you can loosen it up."

"I guess I can pry it out with the screwdriver." Caleb gave a few stout tugs with the blade of the screwdriver and a fancy shaped piece of wood came apart from the lid. It was painted red on the front and sides that faced the lid. In the middle of the piece, on the unpainted side, was a peg hole.

"I wonder what this is supposed to be," Caleb said thoughtfully.

"Caleb, there's only one!" observed Josh. "The clue said there would be two. Where do you think the second one is?"

"I haven't a clue, but let's follow some of the other clues and maybe we'll get a hint as to where the twin is," he replied.

The boys closed the lid of the window seat and began strolling into the next room. Just as they walked through the door Caleb shouted, "I've got it! There's another window seat in here and I just betcha that the twin is in the lid of that one."

They slowly opened the bench to find another curious piece of wood wedged into the lid. The two of them popped the clue out of the lid, and found it was similar in design to the first piece.

"Ya know, if ya look at 'em they don't look like identical twins," observed Joshua. "If ya put them face to face, they go in opposite directions and one piece has more mass to it than the other piece."

"Maybe the 'twins' are the window seats, 'cause they're the same size and look alike. The only difference is, one is in the dining room and the other is in here," said Caleb.

"Okay, so now what are we supposed to do with these two things?" asked Josh.

"Let's put 'em in the bag with the key. And let's look at another clue. *'Parlor décor is always ornate. Ornate I may seem to be, but unattached I may serve thee.'*" he read aloud. "I think that this is the parlor and the only thing that looks ornate is all of the fancy wood design on the wall panel. So let's try moving some of the pieces."

They moved along the wall, trying their best to pull a section of the design loose, when all of a sudden the plaster above the woodwork began to crumble and fall and the entire wooden panel tore loose from the wall. The plaster fell in big chunks and dust flew everywhere. Both boys screamed loudly. Then Josh got hit by a panel and found himself on the floor, under the panel and not able to move very much.

As the dust began to settle, Caleb, covered with chalky white plaster dust and looking like a ghost, called out to his cousin. "Hey, Josh, are you all right? Josh-can you hear me? Josh, where are you?"

Coughing and sputtering, Joshua answered, "I'm here-down here on the floor under all of this stuff! And I don't feel very good. Get me out before I suffocate!"

It took Caleb a few minutes to locate his cousin, and though Joshua wasn't hurt, he was covered with debris. It took Caleb quite a while to get the big pieces of plaster off the panel so that he could free his cousin.

"And you said we wouldn't get into any danger here," sputtered Joshua. "Well, what do you call this? I just about got killed with all of this stuff fallin' on me!"

"I'm sorry Josh," apologized Caleb. "I didn't think this would happen. But hey, look-you're all right, I'm all right. We just need to be a little more careful."

"Well, I'm ready to call it quits! I don't want any more close calls!" said Joshua angrily.

"Come on, will ya, please stick it out with me," begged Caleb. "Please, stay with me a while longer and let's see what we find. Honestly, I can't do this by myself! And I'm plannin' on splitting the treasure, whatever it is, with you. So come on and reconsider."

"Okay, okay," said Josh, calming down a bit. "But I've got a feeling... a feeling I'm going to regret saying I'll stay."

Already looking forward to more investigation, Caleb said, "Good! Now that the panel has fallen down it might make our search a little easier. Let's get the rest of this plaster out of the way and we can look at the panel from the back. That might help us find what we're looking for."

As the boys began moving the plaster pieces out of the way, Josh noticed something strange on the back side, in the middle of the panel.

"Come here, Caleb, look what I've found," he called. "Here are some peg holes and a strange shape cut-out around them."

Caleb studied what Josh had found. "That looks like one of those pieces we found in the window seats, only it's shaped differently. Hey-look over there, there's another peg hole and strange shape cut-out. I think we've found what we need to solve this riddle. Now we just need to push the pieces out of the panel."

Pushing the pieces out of the panel turned into quite a chore for the two of them. Finally Caleb got out his hammer and started beating around the inside edge of the design. In a little while both cut-outs popped out like two puzzle pieces. These pieces were even stranger-looking shapes than the previously found shapes. Once again, when they were put together they didn't fit, but if laid facing one another they appeared to be mirror images. And like the others, they were painted red on one side and natural wood on the other with a peg hole in the middle.

Feeling stumped, Caleb said to Josh, "I'm just going to put these in the bag with the other pieces, and then we can look at another clue and see what's next."

"I don't want any more junk fallin' on me. I want to make that clear right now!" reminded Josh.

"I hear ya, I hear ya loud and clear. All I can say is we'll be more careful. Okay?"

CHAPTER EIGHT

MORE CLUES TO SOLVE

"Okay-what's next?" asked Joshua.

"The next clue has to do with the library and that's where we first came in." instructed Caleb. "So let's go back there and see if we can answer this clue."

The boys did their best to dust themselves off, and returned cautiously to the library. They sat on the leather sofa as Caleb began reading the riddle for the room: *"In the library are many books, so many items can be found. Flames above the hearth protect that what doth lurk in the ground. Bookcases are tricky and seem so tall; one might conceal something quite small. Ivanhoe would know what to do. Behind him Joan of Arc and Robin of Loxley might you find that for which you're looking."*

"That's crazier than the other clues. What on earth is a hearth?" asked Josh.

"A hearth is the floor of a fire place." replied Caleb. "Right now there is no fire in the fireplace so what we probably need to do is clear the ashes away and see what's on the floor of the hearth."

The boys began cleaning, and by the time they had cleared the floor of the hearth, the two of them looked like chimney sweepers-plaster dust in their hair and on their clothing, with smudges of black soot covering their hands and faces. Looking at one another they couldn't help but laugh.

"If my mom saw us now she'd want to hose us down before we could go into the house," laughed Caleb.

"My mom would be mad as a wet hen, and lecturing my ears off about how much she paid for the clothes that I just ruined," Josh said as he tried desperately to clean some of the soot off of his pants.

"Josh," Caleb said excitedly, "this might be what we're looking for. Look at this tile; it doesn't look like the others. The shape and color is different and it has some sort of design painted on it."

While Josh was looking intently at the tile, Caleb jumped up, got his back pack and pulled out a shop towel. "Here, let me wipe it off with this towel, then we can see better just what we have found," he said as he busily scrubbed the hearth floor.

"It's a black fighting lion," exclaimed Josh. "I've seen pictures of them in our history book. Knights would always paint them on their shields or on their flags."

"Yeah, this has to be it. It's the only one that looks different," Caleb said as he looked the hearth over. "Now, how are we going to get it up?"

"I know," he continued, "I'll chisel it out if you'll wipe the loosened grout away as I chisel. Then we should have this piece to add to our collection in no time at all."

Caleb got out his hammer and screwdriver and started chiseling away. Slowly the grout was knocked loose and Joshua was finally able to remove it. Even though it was tile, like the wood pieces it too had peg holes in the back. Caleb placed it in the backpack with the other pieces of the collection.

"Now, what do you think the reference to the books is all about?" Joshua asked.

"Maybe we need to find a book called *Ivanhoe*. The only thing is…this library is full of old smelly books and I don't have a clue as to where to look first. Why don't you look on that shelf to the left and I'll look on this shelf to the right."

"Okay, but it sure is a lot of books. It'll be like looking for a needle in a haystack."

Over an hour of searching passed, and the boys were no closer to finding *Ivanhoe* than when they first began.

"I just don't believe there is such a book," exclaimed Joshua.

"Wait a minute!" said Caleb. "The clue says bookcases are tricky and seem so tall. I bet the book is up high. Like on one of the shelves of that tall bookcase at the end of the room. See-it has stairs going up to a second level, and I bet the book we're looking for is up there."

"Hey, now, wait a minute! Do you think it's safe for us to climb up those stairs? I don't want any more plaster on my head today!"

"Look-the stair and the walkway are metal so surely it's strong enough for the two of us. Come on, I'll go up first and when I get to the walkway, if everything is okay you can follow and help me find the book."

Having offered that piece of advice, Caleb ascended the spiral staircase to the walkway. Reassured, Joshua joined him on the walkway and the twosome hunted shelf after shelf for the elusive *Ivanhoe*. Suddenly Joshua shouted, "I've found *Joan of Arc*!"

Caleb ran over to where Joshua was and sure enough-there was *Joan of Arc* on the shelf. To the right was *Robin of Loxley*, and on the other side was *Ivanhoe*. The boys took the books down and looked through the pages, but they were unable to find clues in any of the three books.

"Now what?" whined a disappointed Joshua.

"If it's not in the books, it must be somewhere on the shelf," said Caleb as he started pulling more books off the shelf. Both boys started feeling around on the shelves, but they found nothing.

"I just thought of something!" exclaimed Caleb. "The clue said 'behind him'…do you think…maybe, just maybe there's a secret panel behind the books? Quick, let's look."

Sure enough, as Caleb ran his hand across the wall behind where the books were standing he heard a clicking noise, and a segment of the wall popped out, revealing a hiding place. Inside the hidden area was a strange carving.

"What on earth could this be? It looks like carved feathers that are red and white. What is all of this stuff supposed to lead to?" Caleb mumbled as he showed what he had just found to Joshua.

"Okay, we found it!" grumbled his cousin. "Now, I'm tired and it's getting late. We've spent the whole day finding these few clues. I say let's go home!"

"But, Josh, we haven't found the treasure yet," said Caleb very disappointedly. "If we stop now, we might not find it before someone else does."

"Wake up, Caleb" argued Josh. "You have the only set of clues! Who else would be silly enough to be out here lookin' for who knows what? You don't even have a clue as to what you're lookin' for! You're just hoping that you'll find something great. Well, I'm tired and with or without you, I'm headin' home."

Knowing that he would not win this argument, Caleb gave in. "Okay, okay. I get the message. But how about spendin' next Friday night at my house? Then we could come over here next Saturday, and maybe we could find the rest of the clues."

"Next Saturday? Maybe, but let's go home now," Josh replied.

As they headed for home, the boys reflected on their adventuresome day. Suddenly Joshua exclaimed, "Just look at us. We've got plaster and soot all over us. How are we going to explain all of this, huh? Huh? Just tell me what we're going to say."

"We're going to say nothing, 'cause they're not going to ask," said Caleb with a grin. "We're almost to the Forked Deer Branch; we'll just jump in for a fun dip like we did the other day. The water will wash the dust and soot off and all we'll have to explain is the wet muddy clothes."

"Oh, you're so sly, Caleb, so very sly," laughed Josh.

So the boys took some time to jump in the Forked Deer Branch and wash each other off as much as possible. Then they biked to Caleb's house where Joshua's sister and parents were just arriving for the cookout.

"What have the two of you been up to?" called Joshua's mother. "Just look at those muddy, wet clothes. Joshua, you know I spend much, too much, money on your clothes, to have you treat them this way."

Caleb laughed, "We just cooled ourselves off in the Forked Deer Branch, but we're going in now to get washed and changed for supper." Then he turned around and gave a wink to Joshua and whispered, "See what I told ya?"

"Yeah," Joshua whispered back, "and you heard the lecture from my mom. I told ya what she'd say, didn't I?"

The rest of the night was spent in merriment as the two families shared an evening of fun, and the two boys made plans for spending the following weekend together. After all, summer was coming to a close and they wanted to have as much fun as they could before the start of school.

Caleb couldn't do anything but dream about the treasure. Questions swirled through his mind. What would the treasure be?

Would it be worth a lot of money? How would he tell his parents about what he had been doing and what he and Josh had found? And most importantly, would Josh hang in there with him to the end?

CHAPTER NINE

NEXT WEEKEND

Early the following Saturday morning, the two boys arrived once again at "The Timbers," where everything was pretty much the same as they had left it the previous Saturday.

"Do you know what one thing is so great about today?" giggled Joshua.

With great surprise in his voice Caleb replied, "No! What makes today so great to you?"

"We don't have to hack our way through all of the underbrush, we don't have to find a way to get into the house, and we've already found a lot of the clues! So today should be smooth sailing. We'll just rush upstairs, grab a few more clues, solve the puzzle and be out of here in a jiff!"

"Right!" Caleb said in a very sarcastic tone of voice, "Yeah, you're right on the first part, but trying to find the rest of the clues may be just as hard or maybe even harder than those we've already found. So let's not get over-confident about today."

"Sometimes…sometimes," mumbled Josh, "you stifle any ray of hope of getting things done quickly. Why do you always have to be the boss and do things so precisely? This could be a lot more fun if we made a game out of it and stopped being so serious."

"Funny you should say that," Caleb snapped back, "Wasn't it you last week who was doing all of the murmuring and wanting to wimp out on this entire adventure?"

"You've got me there! I've had a whole week to think about it, and now I think maybe there is something here and maybe it's worth our time to find all the clues. But I also remember that we could have been killed or hurt real bad by all of that falling plaster and wood paneling. I don't want anything bad to happen to us, but I am excited about us finding whatever you've unearthed in that glass rolling pin. Since it was green glass maybe that means we have the luck of the Irish with us and everything will be okie dokie."

Caleb laughed. "What's the luck of the Irish, and what has that got to do with us?"

"Surely you remember our uncle Marty. Well, he used to brag about the luck of the Irish. Said wearing green, and having shamrocks around the house brings good luck to the people in the house and good luck to anyone wearing green." Then Josh added, "Especially on St. Patrick's Day!"

"Oh, jumpin' lizards, we're wasting time standing here talking. Let's go on inside and look at our next clue."

Once again the two boys entered the house through the French doors of the library. Caleb rummaged through the pockets of his backpack and finally brought out the paper that had the written clues.

"Wow!" he exclaimed. "This could take all day! The fourth clue just says, '*Many porches and rooms to adore, secret panels or a hidden door, the playroom closet holds a surprise, many items I did hide. Find ten and then you can soar up to the third floor for some more.*' And that's the only clue we have...it...it ...it doesn't give even a hint as to where the ten items are. I know one will be in the playroom closet, but where will the other nine be? This is a big house and according to the floor plans the second floor looks like it has a lot more rooms than the first floor has."

"Let's go! Nothing is going to get found with us just sitting here," said Josh.

The boys walked cautiously from the library through the living room and into the foyer where the grand staircase was located. Slowly they began to ascend to the second floor, carefully testing each step, making sure it could hold their weight. Caleb led the way to the first landing.

"Hey, look at this huge clock," commented Caleb. "I wonder why they left this behind. I like chiming clocks! I bet this one makes some sort of deep gonging tones. Hey, Josh, do you think that this would count as part of the second floor?"

"Now how should I know the answer to that?" answered Josh.

"'Cause I was just thinking if this landing was considered part of the second floor, then we might find something in this old clock. You know, I've seen movies where things were hidden in these kinds of clocks." And with that Caleb started looking around the base of the clock trying to find a panel or door that would open.

"Look, this front door opens." He stuck his head inside the clock for a closer look. He found a huge round disc attached to a rod and surmised that was the pendulum. He also saw three chains hanging from the works at the top of the clock all the way down to the bottom of the area into which he was looking.

After surveying the clock parts, Caleb began feeling around the back panel of the box to see if maybe there might be a trap door. Then excitedly he yelled, "Josh, look-there IS a hidden door here!" When he pried it, open, out fell a piece of wood, painted red and shaped like an opened scroll. It was about fourteen inches long and four inches wide.

"This has got to be one of the items we're looking for, 'cause look here, Josh. See, it has three peg holes on the back of it," said Caleb as the two boys examined the new clue. "But it's different because it has these two pegs on the front. Josh, what do you think it is?"

"Well, it looks like a coat rack to me," Josh laughed. "So, I guess this is considered part of the second floor and we just found one of the ten we need to find. What's next on your agenda, my fearless leader?" And with those words Joshua broke out into rolling peals of laughter.

Delighted with this first find, the boys cautiously continued to explore the second floor. Noticing the number of halls and rooms, Caleb wondered, "How will we know where the playroom is?"

"Look at the floor plans that Mr. Timberlake had in the container," Josh reminded him. "You did bring it with you, didn't you?"

"Oh, yeah! Just a minute,.." Caleb said as he searched around in his backpack. "Yep, here it is! The playroom is the first room on the right down this hall. So let's start there first."

With every step the boys took, the floors in the old house creaked, squeaked, and groaned. Often Joshua looked at Caleb and asked, "Do you think it safe for us to go on?" The confident reply was always, "Yes, just watch where you're stepping. If the floor starts to sink, you just jump back and holler." When they arrived at the playroom door, Caleb tried the latch and was surprised to find that the door opened very easily. The boys walked in and looked around.

"Whew! What a big room!" marveled Josh. "The kids who lived here had to have had a great time playing in this room. Look, Caleb, they even have their own porch!"

The two strolled over to the doorway of the porch and peered through the panes. Then Caleb remarked, "Our Aunt Frances who lives in California, had a big screened-in porch upstairs at her house. Our cousins Lois and Peggy played out there all of the time. I thought that was the biggest porch I'd ever seen, but this is zillions of times larger."

Joshua opened the squeaking door, stepped out on the porch and gazed through the screens surrounding the top of the porch. He leaned against the wall trying to get a better look at the grounds around the house, when all of a sudden the wall gave way with a loud groan, and Joshua yelled as he jumped away from it. "That was a close call!" he shouted in a panic as he quickly bounded through the doorway and into the playroom. "I don't think we need to go back out there. Look, that wall is just hanging by the strength of that screen. It looks like it could tear lose at any moment and fall on the ground."

"I…I…I agree!" said Caleb hesitantly. "I think we just need to find the closet and get out of here."

"Closet? Caleb, there is no closet in this room." Josh pointed out.

"Hmmm," Caleb replied, while looking around the room for confirmation of his thought, " I wonder if he was referring to this large cabinet. It's huge and it does have doors on it. Maybe he means this to be a closet."

With those words, Caleb walked over and opened the cabinet. "I bet," he said enthusiastically, "that this is where the kids stored all of their toys when they weren't playing with them."

"Yeah," said Josh. "Look, here is an old jack-in-the-box, and well, it used to be a rubber ball. Look how mushy it's gotten. Can't play with this thing any more. It won't even hold any air."

"Look at that old truck," said Caleb. "It's got a crane on the back and a scoop in the front. I bet this was fun to play with. But wait a minute, we need to find the hidden item so we can have another clue. The paper says there is a surprise hidden in this closet, so we need to look for something that is hidden, not something that's just sitting here."

"I've got an idea," offered Joshua, "Why don't you start on one end checking the walls, door, top, and floor for a hidden opening, and I'll do the same at this end of the closet, okay?"

"Yeah, that sounds good to me," agreed his cousin.

The boys scrutinized every panel and every board in the cabinet. It had two sets of doors, and a small beam about eight inches wide had been placed between each set. As Caleb was searching the floor of the cabinet, he noticed that the floor behind the beam had a small shim going into the back side of the beam.

"That's a rather curious set-up," he thought to himself. "I wonder what would happen if I removed the shim?"

He got a pair of pliers out of his bag and tried to pull the shim out from the beam. After many tries he called out to Joshua, "Look in my bag and bring me that screwdriver and hammer. It looks like we have a bit of work to do to get to the clue."

As before, Caleb used his screwdriver like a chisel. He began hammering away at the shim, hoping to break it off even against the beam. After several tries, he was successful. Once the shim was removed, the board popped up with a smack against the back wall. Inside this space, the boys discovered a box.

"It's just a decorative box," griped Joshua. "What are we to do with a dumb old box?"

Caleb tried to find a way to open the box, but was not successful. Glancing at Joshua, he said, "I believe this is one of those Chinese puzzle boxes. We have to figure out how to open it."

"Where do you start?" asked Joshua.

"I don't know," grunted Caleb, "but I'm going to keep pushing on all of these designs on the box and maybe one of them will give a little and we'll go from there."

Puzzle boxes usually work by having parts that slide in or out in a special sequence, and if you get the right sequence the box will open to reveal its contents. However, many a person has been lured into hours of trying to find the right combination to gain entry. Was this going to happen to Josh and Caleb? Josh watched Caleb as he struggled with the box. All of the time Josh tried to figure out what Caleb's next move would be. It looked to be a difficult task.

Thirty minutes later, Caleb let out a war-whoop. "I got it! Look, this piece here slides in and lets this piece slide over, to the right, and look what I found pressed into the side of the piece that slid over. It's a key!"

"All of that work for another key," Josh says disappointedly. "I would think there would be more than that to find."

"Well, let me keep working with the box now that I got those parts to move. We should still find a way to open this thing," said Caleb.

As Joshua watched, Caleb continued to push in sections of the box. As other sections pop out, new catches appeared and so went the work on the box. Then as Caleb lifted one section of the box up, a keyhole appeared.

"Josh, give me the key, this must be where it goes." Taking the key, Caleb put it into the keyhole and quickly turned it. A lid opened.

"Wow, what a challenge that was!" exclaimed Caleb. Looking into the box, the boys found two strange-looking white pieces of wood carvings.

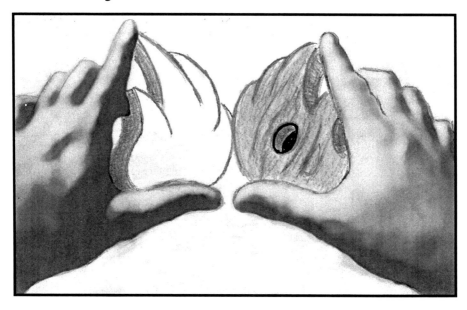

Joshua stared at the two pieces. Then he announced, "Those things look like the very end of a cow's tail." Laughingly he added, "Do you think a cow is part of the puzzle were trying to solve?"

"Who knows what's involved? It gets more mysterious as we go!" replied Caleb.

"Well, how many items have we found so far on this floor?"

"Let's see," Caleb said as he started counting on his fingers, "there's the red scroll carved out of wood, there's the puzzle box, there's the key that we found in the box, and then we have these two weird items. That totals up to five items, so we have five more items to find on this floor. And I just noticed that everything, except the box and the keys, has been painted red or white. I think that's a clue that can help us quickly locate the other items. We'll inspect anything we see that is red or white to see if there's something there for us to take. Okay, let's go on to the next room."

Caleb grabbed up the puzzle box and the two new pieces they'd just found and put them in his backpack. "What are you sticking the puzzle box in your pack for?" Joshua asked with great curiosity.

"Granny likes puzzles and I remember how excited she was the year that we gave her a puzzle box for Christmas. So I think I'll surprise her on her birthday by giving her this one, if that's okay with you."

"Why should I care? It's just a dumb old box!" said Josh with exasperation.

The two boys opened one of the doors leading from the playroom only to find a large bathroom. It contained nothing but a tub, sink, and commode. Nothing looked like it might hold a hidden item, so they closed the door and approached another door. Opening it, they found a large room that they supposed had been used as a bedroom. Remnants of colorful curtains hung from the windows as did a lot of cobwebs and dust. Wallpaper, which was peeling from the walls near the ceiling, was still colorful and showed children at play. "This must have been the children's bedroom," sighed Joshua. "I wish my room was this big."

Finding no clues in the bedroom, Caleb said, "Doesn't look like there's anything here, so let's go look In another room."

Returning to the hallway, they decided to look in the room across the hall. It was another bedroom, also very empty except for peeling wallpaper and ragged curtains. After finding one more, empty bedroom, they returned to the mezzanine and stared down at the staircase they had ascended earlier.

"Wow, that's a long ways down to the floor," Joshua said with a bit of a shaky voice. "But those banisters look like they would be loads of fun to slide down. Shall we take a little time out and slide down to the first floor?"

"Not right now. We need to find these other clues." The tone of his cousin's voice gave Joshua the notion that Caleb was terribly disgusted with the fact that they hadn't found any more clues since they left the playroom. Focused on investigating, Caleb continued, "Hey, see that door over there? Let's go see what's on the other side of it."

They crossed the mezzanine and made a right turn heading toward a door that exited onto a balcony in the front of the house. Looking out through the door, they noticed that part of the railing had fallen off and was dangling from the balcony. Right away they backed up and decided this was one place they didn't need to explore. However, near the balcony was another door standing ajar. They slowly opened it and entered a really neat bathroom.

"What a sight!" exclaimed Josh. "Caleb, look at the size of that tub! Four people could get in that tub at one time."

"You think that's something? Come around here and look at this room!" called Caleb, who had walked beyond the bathroom.

Josh walked around the wall into what appeared to be the master bedroom. At the far wall was a large platform extending into the room, looking like it may have been where the bed sat at one time. "Now that's some place to put a bed!" observed Josh.

"Yes," said Caleb, focusing on the opposite wall, "but I'm more interested in this wall. Turn around here and look at what I see."

Josh followed Caleb's directions, and studied the wall. "I see the initials 'J T' with a circle around them, and some unusual wood carvings jutting off of the circle. Kind of makes it look real fancy," he told Caleb.

"Yeah," said Caleb, "but it also looks a lot like some of the stuff we've been finding when we follow the riddles and clues. Let's see if any of it is loose enough to pull away from the wall and add to our collection."

The boys pulled and twisted every piece, trying to remove each one from its present location. Finally, two pieces came away from the wall and the boys discovered that, like the other pieces of their collection, each of these had a peg hole smack dab in the middle of the back.

"Hurray," shouted Jacob, "now we can go to the third floor!"

"Oh, no, we can't," argued Caleb. "We need two more items."

"Two more," Josh sighed. "I'm getting tired of looking. Oh, beans, you can't count! Those two items only count up to seven and I do believe that it says we have to find ten items before we can soar! And we don't even have any clues except that the items are on the second floor somewhere."

"Onward," shouted Caleb. "Three more should be easy to find. Let's check out the other rooms." With those words, Caleb took off through the door that led to the mezzanine. When he got to the corner, he made a right turn down the hall. This hallway turned out to be much darker than the other hallways, because there were no windows.

"Josh, you check out the first room," directed Caleb. "I'm going down the hall and check out the second room. If you find anything, give a yell, will ya?"

"You can bet on it!" replied Josh.

The boys soon returned, because all they found in the two rooms were ragged window drapes, lots of dust and cobwebs, torn or fallen wallpaper and empty closets. As they met again in the hall, they shrugged their shoulders and shook their heads in disbelief that they found nothing.

"I'm stumped," said Caleb. "Without any more clues, where do we look?"

"We didn't check that door in the middle of the mezzanine," Josh pointed out.

"What door?" asked Caleb.

"Follow me," said Joshua excitedly. "I'll show you which door." Josh led Caleb to a door in the middle of the mezzanine at the top of the grand staircase.

Slowly he opened it and peeked inside. Caleb looked over Josh's shoulder and exclaimed, "Josh, it's black as tar in here. Let me get a flashlight and we'll be able to safely look around."

"That's better," said Josh. "But could ya just shine it on the floor, 'cause I don't want to step in any holes or trip over any lose boards or other junk."

"There, the floor looks safe," Caleb remarked. "Now I think we need to shine some light around the walls and look for some clues. Josh, keep a sharp eye out for anything that looks unusual."

"Golly be, Caleb," exclaimed Josh, after looking around. "This here is another bathroom! How many bathrooms do you think they have in a house this size?"

"Who cares," grumbled Caleb. "Instead of worrying about how many bathrooms there are, you should be focusing on finding more clues. Okay, cuz."

"Hey, look up there above the tub! It's some more of those red curly design things," shouted Joshua. "I think we can stand on the tub rim and reach them," he said excitedly. "These are our final pieces, aren't they?"

Two eleven year olds balance themselves on the side of the tub while stretching upward to pull at the design. Josh held the flashlight and Caleb pulled hard on each piece. Finally they were rewarded with two pieces that looked like part of a fleur-de-lis. But the center section fell off and was actually two halves that were put together.

"Now what are we going to do?" sighed Joshua. "We only need three pieces, and here we stand with four pieces in our hands!"

Needing more light, the two of them gathered up their pieces and carefully made their way out into the hall.

"Let's look at the back side of all of the pieces," suggested Caleb. "Hey, they have a hole in the back like all of the others, so maybe we had better keep all four!"

"Well, maybe Mr. Timberlake was counting the key and the puzzle box as one," mused Josh.

"Who knows what Mr. Timberlake was thinking when he put all of this together. I'm beginning to think he was a bit of a nut. But who cares as long as we find the treasure that he's hidden," said Caleb.

"That's okay with me," agreed Josh. "Now, where is the stairway to the third floor?"

Caleb pulled out the floor plans and studied them intently. Finally he announced excitedly, "Look at this crazy layout! It looks like the stairs are down this hallway and behind the bathroom." Wrinkling his forehead, he said to Josh, "They sure built their homes in a crazy way, don't you think?"

"Yeah, but this whole thing has been crazy from the start, so let's get hopping up those stairs." Josh headed for the stairs as Caleb stuffed the plans back in his bag, and ran to catch up with his cousin.

CHAPTER TEN
WHAT'S ON THE THIRD FLOOR

As the boys emerged from the stairwell, they stood in amazement. Before them was a huge room that ran the full width of the entire house. There were four balconies off of the room, two on each side of the house. The wall at one end of the room was covered with beautifully carved paneling from ceiling to floor. The opposite end of the room had a mirrored wall. In front of the wall was a large, old-fashioned soda fountain complete with a carved wooden counter. The wood floor was still very polished in areas.

"Gee," exclaimed Josh, his eyes big as saucers. "What do you think they used this room for?"

"You got me! All I can say is that whoever the kids were that lived here, well, they must have been able to have some fun parties with all of this space. And their parents wouldn't have been bothered by the noises since they were probably all the way down on the first floor."

"Hey, that would be a blast!" said Josh excitedly. "We could have the entire scout troop up here and invite another troop to join us for a sleepover. Wow, wouldn't that be great! Well, it would be great if we owned the place."

"Well," replied Caleb, "we'd better quit daydreaming and get to solving the sixth riddle. It says, 'Mirror, mirror on the wall, what behind me must I see to gain access and relieve my stress.' And then it goes on to say, 'The Western sun shines a ray of light, open a door and behold the sight. If you can't figure this one out, you may have to sit and pout.' So let's start by looking in the mirror."

"All I see behind us is that big paneled wall," observed Joshua.

"Okay," said Caleb. "Let's look at the floor plans and see what we're missing.""Hey, there's another room on the other side of that wall. That's what we have to find! We have to find where the door is!"

Running over to the wall, Joshua looked it over carefully and then reported, "There are no door knobs over here! Not a one and I don't see any hinges either."

"I guess the door is hidden and that's why it says we'll have to sit and pout if we can't figure it out. In a movie I saw, I remember that the library had a mysterious door ... let's see if ... if I remember right, there was a hidden lever on the desk, which would open the door. Yeah, it was a statue, and when you pulled on its head, it opened the door!"

Looking around the room, Josh said, "I don't see any statues or desks around here. So what's your next bright idea?"

"Let's examine the wall with our hands and see if we can find something that feels like a door. Or maybe we can find something that looks like a trigger to open the door."

Caleb started on one side of the wall and Joshua took the other side. They examined every little nook and cranny of the paneling, hoping to find some clue as to where the door or its trigger mechanism might be. But, alas, they found nothing.

"All right," Caleb announced, "let's assume that the door is in the middle of the wall. Let's just start pushing in on the wall and knocking on it 'til we find something."

"Knocking on the wall?" questioned Joshua. "Knocking on the wall? What do you think is going to happen? Do you think a butler is going to answer the knock and let us in?"

"No", said Caleb rolling his eyes, "but I've seen movies where detectives find secret openings and hidden doors by knocking on the wall. If it sounds hollow, then you know that you've found the door."

"You and your TV or movie programs, you know it don't always happen that way in real life," said Josh.

"Well, humor me this one time. We might get lucky, you know?"

"Okay," said Josh, without conviction. He began walking alongside the wall, hitting it with his fists.

"Sounds solid to me, sounds very solid." Suddenly, instead of a solid thud he heard an empty whap.

"Gee whiz, I think I've found the door. Now what?" he asked, turning to Caleb.

"My remembrances of old movies paid off, huh?"

"Yeah, yeah, yeah. Now, how are we going to open it?"

"Let's try pushing on all of the woodwork around what sounds like the door."

The two of them thumped and pushed, thumped and pushed for a long time with no results.

Slightly discouraged, Josh said, "I'm tired, why don't we take a break and eat lunch. Then we can think about this a little more clearly."

"Yeah, I'm with you on that," agreed Caleb. Let's sit over there by the counter. That way we can look at the whole wall at once while we're eating."

The boys walked across the room and sat on the floor, leaning against the counter while they ate their lunches and washed it all down with bottled water. As they ate, they eyed the paneled wall and tried to figure out how in the world they were going to get the door open.

"Caleb," asked Joshua, "is that all that the sixth riddle says?"

"No, the last part of the clue says 'Somewhere you'll find my moniker, take it with you, surely there's a proper place to affix such a thing.' Maybe we should solve the seventh clue first."

"Okay, but what's a moniker?" Josh asked his cousin.

"Oh, come on now, surely you know what a moniker is!" exclaimed Caleb.

"Maybe you do, but it's a new word for me. So explain away, fellow."

"Well," asked Caleb, "if I told you that your moniker is Joshua Scott Rice, what would I be telling you?"

"You mean a moniker is your name."

"That's right. Now, do you see 'Jacob Timberlake' written anywhere in this room?"

Joshua stood up and looked all around. "Nope," he replied, "but I do see TIMBERLAKE carved in some nice lettering on the front of this counter!"

"Whoa…I didn't see that! You've got good eyes after all!" Caleb jumped up, and the two boys tried hard to remove the name from the front of the counter. Finally Caleb whipped out his screwdriver and used it to pry the name off. It wasn't easy, but in a little while they had the name off and placed it in the bag with the rest of the items they had found.

"Hey, Josh," Caleb said to his cousin. "Look what's on the panel where we just removed the name. There's a button there. Let's push it and see what happens!"

Caleb pushed the button. A moment later the boys heard a groaning noise, then a shake and rumble as the hidden door at the other side of the room slid into the wall, revealing a new room for them to explore.

"Wow, am I glad that you found Timberlake's name on the counter!" said Caleb. If we'd never gone on to the rest of the clue, we would still be wondering how to get that door open." Caleb gave Josh a high-five and the two laughed as they ran to the opening. "Now, where's the next door that we're suppose to open?" asked Joshua.

"The clue says, "The Western sun shines a ray of light, open a door and behold the sight. Hmm, the light is shining from that window and it's shining to the right side of the room," Caleb expressed after thinking a bit, "so if we climb over some of this stuff we'll probably find another door over that way."

"Well, they sure left a lot of junk in this place," observed Joshua. "Do you suppose that the family didn't know how to get into here either?"

After climbing around and over some boxes and trunks and odd pieces of furniture, they finally reached the wall on the right side of the room. Sure enough, there was a door.

"Let's hope it's not locked," Caleb said as he reached for the door knob. "Aha-it's unlocked!" He swung the door open wide.

There before them with the sunbeams shining brightly upon it was a large cabinet with fancy carved scrollwork covering both halves of the double doors. It was similar to what Josh and Caleb had already found, and it too was painted white. They knew this had to be what they were looking for. Once again with the aid of the screwdriver they pried two pieces off and added them what they already had.

"Now, finally we're ready for the last clue!" exclaimed Caleb joyfully.

"Hurray, now we can go--huh, where are we going, Caleb?" asked Josh.

"To the basement we go, and to our reward for all of this craziness."

As fast as they could, they clambered back over all the trunks, furniture and boxes, and then headed straight for the stairs. Now in the mood for fun, Caleb said, "Okay, Josh let's slide on the banisters all the way to the bottom. You take the right side and I'll take the left. When I say 'go', the race is on!"

With thrilling yelps the two slid down to the bottom. Joshua actually slid all of the way off and on to the floor, then sat up and laughingly said, "Hey, we need to do that again."

"Not right now," Caleb said has he crawled off the banister. "We've got to find our way to the basement and locate the last few pieces that we need to solve this mystery of The Timbers."

CHAPTER ELEVEN

AT LAST THE TIMBERLAKE TREASURE

"Where's the stairs to the basement?" asked Joshua as he looked around.

"Guess I'll have to look at the plans again," Caleb replied as he put his backpack down and started rummaging through it once more. "Let's see, it looks like the stairs to the basement are just inside the kitchen door. So, follow me. I think it's over by the closet where we started all of this. I want to find these last clues in a hurry because I'm anxious to know what were going to share."

"Share? Did you say share?" asked Josh.

"Yes! You don't think I'm going to hog all the treasure to myself, do you? I planned all along to share it with you. After all, you were brave enough to give up two of your Saturdays to help me with this venture. So sure, I'm going to share it with you!"

"Wow! Let's see how fast we can do this!" exclaimed a happy Josh.

Once inside the kitchen, the boys located the stairwell leading down to the basement. It was completely dark, so Caleb got out the flashlights and they headed down the steps slowly and carefully. At the bottom, the boys found themselves in a large hallway. On the right side of the hall were two doors which, upon investigation, turned out to lead to bathrooms. On the left at the very end of the hall was a gate leading into a very dark room on the other side. "It looks too scary in there," said Josh with a shaky voice. "Let's explore elsewhere."

Going back down the hall and turning left the boys were awestruck with what they found. They were in a huge room, almost the size of the room on the third floor. Near the ceiling were windows that encompassed the perimeter of the room. The windows gave ample enough light for the boys to see without the flashlights.

At the far end of the room were two bowling lanes and tables and chairs. To the left were several chairs and tables and a dartboard was affixed to the wall. To their left, parallel with the bathrooms were two billiard tables. "Can you even imagine how much fun it would be to live in a place like this?" asked Josh in tones of wonder.

"No, Josh, it's hard to imagine. But boy, what fun it must be to have enough money to be able to live in a place like this. That Mr. Timberlake must have been a really rich guy. But he must not have liked his family very much; else he wouldn't have done this, you know…give someone else a chance to find all of his fortune. He must have been a very unhappy guy, but he's about to make us very happy, huh!"

"Well, where do we start?" questioned Joshua.

Getting out the clues, Caleb read, "The first part of the seventh clue is, 'under the green between the pockets, lies a prize if you can unlock it.' So look around and see if you can find something green."

The two began a diligent search of the entire room, looking for something green. The colors in the room were anything but green, so after a few turns about the room Joshua announced, "The only green in this room is on those two pool tables over there."

"Hey, that makes sense," said Caleb, "because it says 'under the green between the pockets' and pool tables have pockets. Let's see which table is hiding the clue!"

Crawling under the first table the boys found nothing. Then they crawled under the second table and found a crazy- looking device on the underside. The device that looked like a box was seven inches by eight inches and made of wood. It was about one inch thick and had a notch cut into the side of the box and into the table on each side of it as if something needed to slip into each of the notches. As Caleb examined the device, he noticed that there were several objects that slid back and forth however they were attached to a rod that only allowed them to move in one back and forth direction. Some moved vertically while others moved horizontally. This caused some pieces to have their movement blocked by others.

"Josh," called Caleb, "you better get under here with me and see if you can figure this contraption out."

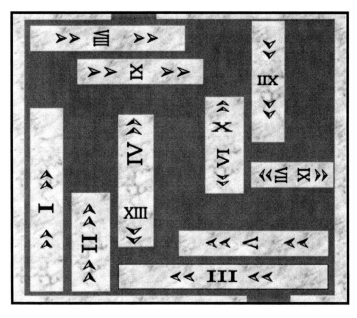

Crawling under and looking up at the contraption, Joshua exclaimed, "This is like one of those sliding picture puzzles. You're going to have to keep sliding the pieces around until you can get one piece to slide into that opening and then do the same thing to get a piece to slide into this other opening. Then I bet the whole thing will come out and we'll get to whatever it is we're supposed to get!"

"Look-there are markings on these pieces. Hold the flashlight so I can get a better look at them."

Each slider was marked with directional arrowheads. The boys also noticed letters between the arrowheads. This was to them a very perplexing situation.

"Hey, remember when we did that fun project in math class last year?" Josh said with a sparkle in his eyes. "You know, where we were working with Roman numerals? Don't these letters remind you of Roman numerals?"

"You're right, they do! Let's see if I can arrange them in numerical order." Caleb started moving the slider with the 'I' etched on it, but it could only move so far before becoming blocked. He worked persistently, and finally figured the proper sequence in order to open the way for the proper piece to slide from the box into the slot in the table.

"Hey, it's not going in very easy!" exclaimed a frustrated Caleb. "What should I do now? Shall I get my hammer and bang it into the slot?"

"No, I wouldn't do that," cautioned Josh, "you might break it. Why don't you just push a little harder? If you need for me to help you push, I will."

Groaning with effort, Caleb continued to push on the piece. Just then, he felt it slide in and he also heard a loud click.

"Wow! That does it! We've got the first piece to go into the slot," Caleb shouted jubilantly. "Whew! What do you know about that? We're half-way there!"

Caleb continued working the slides in numerical order. In a little while he said to Josh, "look! That clears the way for the XIII to slide all of the way out through the other slot. Oh, no," he groaned, "this is going to be another tough one." Just as he got the words out of his mouth, the piece slid like it was greased. With a loud click it too settled into place.

"We've done it! We've done it!" laughed Caleb. At that moment, the entire box dropped onto the floor and to boy's surprise a knight's helmet was set into the other side of the box.

"Now what do you think were supposed to do with this thing?" Caleb asked his cousin.

"I guess you just need to add it to everything else we've collected. The question is, how many more things do we have to get before we get the final object that we've been working so hard for?"

Reading the letter, Caleb replied, "The next clue says, 'Ten pins and alleys, cats and feathers, what you need is in plain sight between two balls I guess you might.' So this should be easy. Pins and alleys must refer to the bowling area. But what are cats and feathers?"

"Let's look! It said it's in plain sight between two balls. Looking around the room, Josh remarked, "I don't see any balls, do you?"

"No, but there's where the two balls would roll from" Caleb pointed out, "and there's that black lion again. I would call a lion a cat, wouldn't you?"

"Yeah, and I guess that fancy work on each side of it could be called feathers of a sort," laughed Josh. "Let's get them off quick!"

They removed the two fancy white moldings from around the lion and then they began jumping up and down in a victory dance. "We have found all of the clues! We've found everything! Hurray, hurray, hurray!"

Joyfully they slapped their hands together, locked elbows and swung each other around until they fell down in laughter. "We've done it! We've done it! Now the treasure is ours!"

As he lay laughing on the floor, Caleb looked up at the ceiling. Suddenly he sat straight up and shouted, "Oh, no, it's not all over! We have one more clue to follow. It says, 'Now you must go through the gate for that is where you'll find your fate. I have helped you all I can; now you solve the rest of the plan. For if you solve this mystery all the possessions I value are yours to take.' Get up, Josh, and let's finish the task. It shouldn't take much longer."

Weak from the frolicking, Joshua reluctantly got up and said in a panting voice, "Oh, just point me to the gate."

Then Caleb pointed out, "The only gate I have seen in this house is at the end of the hall down here.

"Oh, no," quivered Josh, "not that gate!"

The two of them returned to the gate, and once again they peered through the bars.

"Yuk, it is unbelievably dark in there," commented Josh. "I don't like the dark, especially when it's dark in a place I've never been before. We don't know what's in there. You know, it could be a den of snakes. Remember in that movie how Indiana Jones dropped down in that tomb looking for something and it turned out that everything had snakes crawling all over it?" Shuddering, he added, "I don't like snakes!"

"Hey, you take the hand-held flashlight and I'll take the hat flashlight, and we'll go in together," replied his cousin. "If we see any snakes we'll run right back out here. I don't like snakes either, Josh, and I wish you hadn't reminded me of that Indiana Jones story. It gives me the willies, but we can't get to the treasure without the risk. So buck up, and let's dive in and put an end to the adventure!"

With a gulp so loud you could have heard it upstairs, Joshua said to Caleb, "You go first and I'll…. I'll be right….yeah, right behind you."

Slowly they opened the creaky gate, surprised that it was not rusted shut. Shining their flashlights on the floor and then the ceiling, they made sure there were no snakes in the room. Satisfied, they began to take stock of what was there.

The first thing they noticed was the many shelves filled with bottles, all covered with spider webs.

"Hey…you know what this is, Josh? It's a wine cellar!" exclaimed Caleb.

"And just where have you been in a wine cellar before?" asked Josh.

"I've never been in one, but I saw one on TV the other night in an episode of 'Murder She Wrote'. It looked a lot like this one, except without the cobwebs, and those huge wooden barrels," he said, pointing them out to Josh.

"Look at that design painted on the front of each one. You know what that design is?"

Josh shook his head.

"Oh, it's a….uh….not a shield, but a…uh…oh, families used to have one made to represent their heritage. I remember the one for granny's family. It had a big shield with blue dolphins jumping across it. But she didn't call it a shield, she said it was a…a…family crest! That's it- the family crest! This must be the Timberlake family crest."

The boys continued through the room, flashing their lights in every nook and cranny. Suddenly, Caleb noticed a vat that didn't have the family crest upon it like the rest of the vats in the room. Instead, the vat displayed a carving that was shaped just like the crest, but void of any design or color. Poking out of the crest were numerous wooden pegs.

"Josh-look!" exclaimed Caleb. "I think that the pieces we've been collecting might fit right there on those pegs. Least ways, that would make more sense as to why there are holes in the back of every piece we've found."

"Help me gather this stuff," Caleb says as he dumped all of the pieces from his backpack onto the floor. "Then we can figure out what piece goes where in this crest."

"How about starting with these two white pieces that look like the end of a cow's tail?" asked Josh.

"Yeah, that's a perfect fit," Caleb said excitedly.

Then Josh got to giggling about the cow's tail and asked, "Are you in a red mood yet?"

"What's got into you Josh?" Caleb laughed.

"Oh, I got these two red pieces that look like someone's outstretched arms. How about finding a place to plug them in," Josh smirked, and then broke into hilarious laughter.

"Great," said Caleb, "see how well they fit!" He was trying hard to quit laughing but every time he looked at Josh he would start snickering again. So he looked around at the pieces on the floor and said, "Now, Josh, can you hand me those four red pieces that we found in the bathroom. Uh…yes, perfect fit again!"

"Caleb," said Josh after studying the design for a while, "I bet this feather looking plume of red and white, goes right there at the top middle. See how the shape of the carving looks just like the shape of this plume."

"Yes, siree, you are so right. And that red scroll that we found in the clock has to go right here at the bottom of the crest," said Caleb, as if he were the only one that could see that it was a very evident next move. "Now, how about those two fancy little pieces, you know the ones with the upward swing. Doesn't it kind of remind you of two leaves?"

"Yes it does," agreed Josh. As he picked up more pieces, he added, "And here are four more pieces that are painted white."

"Hey," shouted Josh with excitement in his voice. "I know now why that red scroll has some peg out front."

"Oh, yeah, smarty pants?" snipped Caleb. "Are you going to give me a clue? Or are you going to keep me in the dark?"

"Don't be silly," Josh laughed. "I just wanted you to know that I found something out before you for once. And it makes me feel good." With those words and a big grin on his face, he handed Caleb the 'Timberlake' name plate. "See, his moniker goes right there on the pegs just as neat as can be! Don't you think so?"

"Okay, cuz," Caleb said apologetically, "is there another item you have an idea of where it should go?"

With a great deal of satisfaction Jacob took the helmet and said, "The knight's helmet must go here under the plume."

"I agree," said Caleb. After putting the helmet in place, he then picked up the shield and placed it smack dab in the middle of the crest. "There now, everything is back in place and the crest is complete. Now what's supposed to happen?" Caleb wondered.

The two of them stood and stared at the crest. Then they shined their lights trying to see if there was anything else that they might have missed. With exasperation, Josh sighed, "You know, this is pretty dumb. We've spent two whole days running all over this place solving clues and picking up pieces for this crest, and what does it get us?"

"Tired and brain dead!" Caleb replied. "Let's just think for a minute or two. Mr. Timberlake had to have had some special reason to have hidden all of those pieces in so many places. And he had no way of knowing that whoever found that glass thing would take it seriously. And all of the pieces might not have stayed hidden. I mean, well, just think about it. Anyone could have destroyed some of the pieces that were in plain sight without even knowing what they were doing."

"Yeah, you're right about that. So what pieces weren't in plain sight?"

Caleb started pondering the events of the two days they spent plundering through the house. "Let's look at the crest and work our way down from the top. One and two would be the cow's tail pieces. Third would be the helmet plume. Then four and five would be the two red pieces that were embedded in the lids of the window seats. Six would be the knight's helmet and seven and eight would be the two white pieces that were hidden in the closet on the third floor. Nine would be the shield that was hidden in the hearth of the fireplace, and ten would be the red scroll from the grandfather clock on the landing." Then he said confidently, "Those are the only pieces that were so hidden that they would still have been in place, unless…unless the house had burnt down to the ground."

"Whoa, you forgot the key! You know-the very first item we found. And we've never used it for anything. There's not been one clue that involved a key, except the puzzle box, and we found its key hidden within. So, do you suppose we need to use the key?"

"I don't know. Where would we use it? We'd have to find a keyhole. A keyhole would be a clue for us to use that key."

The boys went down on their knees, and examined the entire vat. Then they looked the cellar over to see if there was a keyhole somewhere else. Of course, with just the light of their flashlights it was an awesome task.

Finally the two of them gave up. Then Caleb got an idea. "Why don't we just push real hard on each of the pieces of the crest? Just maybe one of them will trigger an opening or a keyhole somewhere."

"Caleb," Joshua said after a great deal of thought, "Why push all of them? Don't you think one piece might be more important to Mr. Timberlake than all the rest?"

"Say, I think you're right. If I were Mr. Timberlake, I would think my name was the most important piece." So Caleb pushed hard against the TIMBERLAKE name and also against the scroll behind it but nothing happened.

"I know, the largest piece that we found completely intact was the shield in the middle, so let's press hard against that. In fact I'm so sure about this that I want you to press hard with me," he said. "Two working together is stronger than one. I know that from one of my Sunday school lessons. So on the count of three, push with all of your might."

Sure enough, when the two of them pressed hard against the shield with the lion silhouette on it, there was a loud click and the entire front section of the vat swung open to reveal a concealed room. Pulling the front section all of the way open the boys shined their lights inside and discovered a door in the middle of a wall. On the door was - you guessed it - a keyhole right above the latch.

"Josh, dig out that key, I want you to have the pleasure of unlocking that door for us," Caleb said excitedly.

Scrabbling around on the floor where they had dumped all of the stuff from the backpack, Joshua looked for the key. He felt around on the floor and inside the backpack several times then looked up at Caleb with a shrug of his shoulders and announced, "I can't find the key."

"What? What do you mean, you can't find the key? We've kept everything right here in this backpack, so everything should be accounted for." With that Caleb stomped on the floor and then began his own search. "It's just got to be here!" he said frantically.

"That was the first thing we found. Did you take it out of the bag and leave it at home?" questioned Joshua.

"No! Of course not!" said Caleb emphatically. "But wait a minute…I…I …yeah, I know where it is. Look here," he picked up the backpack and just inside the large pocket on the front was another, smaller pocket with a Velcro closure. "It was so small that I put it here for safe keeping. And it's safely in my hand now," Caleb confessed, "and I'm giving it to you. So go on and unlock the door before something else goes wrong."

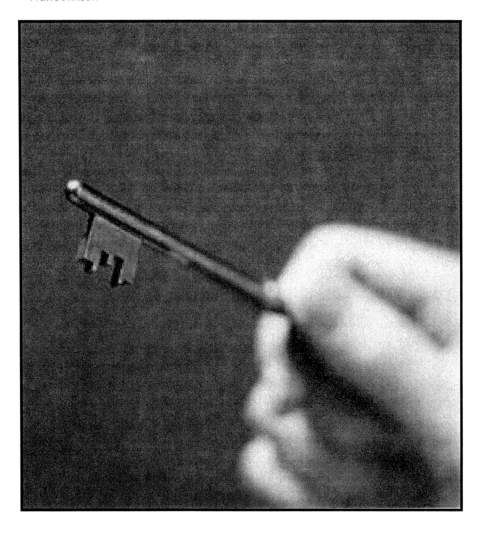

While Caleb held a light, Joshua stepped inside the vat and unlocked the inner door. Slowly he opened the door and the boys peered inside. To their surprise, the entire vat was a small hidden room containing shelves that were filled with all sorts of antique clocks, three large stamp albums, five albums filled with coins and currency, and a metal box about the size of a small briefcase. The boys were stunned; these were not the kind of treasures they had conjured up in their daydreaming minds. They were thinking of gold coins and bags of money. What were they going to do with this stuff?

"Well I'm disappointed, how about you?" Caleb said sadly while opening up the metal box. "Look here, just a bundle of old paper money, some certificates, a letter addressed to The Finder Of My Treasure, a letter addressed to Robert C. Copeland Esquire, Attorney, and a deed to The Timbers. La-de-da."

Joshes grunted in agreement. "La-te-da is right. Now what are we going to do with all of this stuff that we've found it?"

"I think it's time to let my dad in on what we've been spending all of our time doing the past two Saturdays. We're going to have to ease into this explanation because I think this is a lot bigger than he can understand all at once. So I've just gotten an idea on how to handle all of this."

"Oh, yeah?" said Joshua. "Well, how about tuning me in to this great plan of yours?"

"It's easy," explained Caleb. "We'll pack this metal box into the back pack. Close the door and lock it, and put the key back in that little Velcro pocket of the backpack. Next, we'll close the vat door and secure it in place. Then we'll take all of the parts of the crest off and pack them in the backpack and go home."

Scratching his head and looking very perplexed, Josh said, "Then what's going to happen when we get to your house?"

"Well… (Gulp)…I'm going to try to ease my dad into a conversation about how we've been spending our time. About how Uncle Chip let me have that thing I dug up and how we just followed the instructions that were inside."

Then, seeming to be stumped for the first time in his life, Caleb when on to say, "I…I…I have all of these items. Well, the clues and the metal box, so I can show him and get him to advise us of what we should do next. Gee wilier, I didn't think it would be this complicated to find a treasure and keep it. Did you?"

"No." admitted Joshua, "but I think it's wise for us to let your dad in on what's been happening. He's very smart about these things and that makes me feel better. My dad would box my ears and yell at me. Probably call me an idiot for attempting such a thing. But Caleb," Josh said confidently, "you have a great dad, that's why I like to spend so much time at your house. Your dad will guide us in the right direction and he'll probably want to join in on the adventure. You probably should have told him about this last week."

"Hey, Josh, you're so right," admitted Caleb with a big smile on his face. "My dad is great, and you're right, if I had told him about all of this last week he would probably have come out here and helped us. Let's get out of here right now. I can hardly wait to get home and see what he has to say."

CHAPTER TWELVE

FACING THE MUSIC AT HOME

Early in the evening, the boys arrived at Caleb's house to find his dad and Uncle Chip watching a baseball game on TV. The boys looked at one anther, shrugged their shoulders and shook their heads – halfway in disgust and halfway in relief. Rolling his eyes, and motioning with his head, Caleb directed Joshua to go to the dining room. In the dining room, without any conversation, the boys took everything out of the backpack and stacked them in neat piles. At the head of the table they placed all of the documents that had come from the container in Uncle Chip's yard. Then they made a pile of all of the items that the clues led them to find. And finally they placed the metal box that they had retrieved from the hidden room.

"Now what do you think we should do?" questioned Joshua.

"I've been thinking about it all of the way home," sighed Caleb. "And I don't really know how to go about telling my dad about this whole thing, but I'm glad that Uncle Chip is here because he can vouch for the first part of our story." Then looking very disgusted Caleb added, "Knowing my dad, he'll think that we need to give all of this stuff that we've found back to Uncle Chip since that container I dug up was found on his property."

"I guess we better get this over with right now," said Josh, "while your dad is in such good spirits. Least way he sounds that way right this minute."

"Of course he's in good spirits, his team is winning. That always puts a grin on his face and makes him slap happy." After a very big sigh Caleb said, "I may as well go face the music. Hanging out in here isn't making it any easier to talk to him about what we've been up too. Come on, Josh, let's join the game and during the commercial, or something, well, maybe I can get a word in about this stuff. Just maybe there will be enough time to squeeze in our story."

Caleb and Joshua entered the den where Uncle Chip and his dad were excitedly engrossed in the baseball game.

"Look at Francoeur run! He's headed for home plate!" shouted Uncle Chip. "Those Braves have got to win today. They just have too," answered Caleb's dad. "We can't have the Giants beating our Braves! Hang in there, guys!"

It was not long before Joshua and Caleb also found them selves excited about the game. The Atlanta Braves were Caleb's favorite baseball team, and he sure wanted them to win. One hour later they watched as Chipper Jones took the plate and with bases loaded made a home run, bringing the game to an end. The Brave beat the Giants eleven to four.

The den was full of cheers and excitement as the foursome celebrated their team's win. Then, Uncle Chip got up and headed towards the door. "It's about time for me to head home," he smiled. "Millie will be upset if I spend the night over here, too. I've already spent most of the day!"

"Uh…w-w-wait, Uncle Chip," said Caleb nervously, "I need your opinion about something. So, can you stay for a few minutes more?"

"Sure, but your dad always has better insight than I do. Are you sure you want my opinion, too?"

"Yes," Caleb said politely, "because it all started last week in your yard."

"Did you say, in my yard?" Chip asked with a surprised look on his face.

"Yes, sir," Caleb said as he began to relate to George and Chip all of the events that had taken place over the past couple of weekends. He told them about all of the things they had found and then concluded, "We brought the metal box with its letter home with us. And also we brought all of the keys and parts of the crest. We did that just in case someone else went in the house, so they wouldn't be able to get into the secret room." Then looking at Uncle Chip he said, "You know last week, when you said I could have that thing I dug up? Now that it's worth something are you going to ask for it back?"

Chip reached over and rustled his fingers through Caleb's hair, "No, Caleb, you more than earned what you've found. The question is, is all of this legal?"

The four of them went into the dining room and looked at all of the items laid out on the table. George picked up the maps, floor plans and other documents and studied them as thoroughly as possible. Meanwhile, Chip read through the document that was found in the metal box. Then George, looking very dumbfounded said, "I'm finding it hard to believe all of this. I know that I'm looking at all of the stuff you've brought home. And it's all very real…but only a crazy person would do such!"

"Hold up, brother-in-law," says Chip, "crazy rich people are called eccentric, and they can get away with it because they're so rich."

"Okay, Chip, Josh, and Caleb, let's get in the car and drive out there. I want the two of you to show us the hidden room and then I'll decide what we're going to do after that. Chip, I know that this has been an exciting adventure for the boys, however, unless we can find that lawyer and make sure everything is on the up and up, well, someone may want to get the boys up on charges of trespassing. After all, that is private property they've been rummaging through and there are laws that prevent that type of intrusion."

The four of them got into the car and Caleb gave his father directions on how to get there. Once inside the gate Caleb and Joshua led them down into the basement. George had brought a large flood light along, and with more light the wine cellar was well lit. The boys led them to the vat and quickly assembled the crest on the front. Then they were able to open the inner door and there for all to see were the clocks, stamp albums, coin books, and lots of dust and cobwebs.

George was very perplexed by it all. "Chip what do you think we should do?"

"I say that we lock everything up again, and go back to the house and examine the contents of that metal box more closely. Come Monday, I think we better contact your lawyer first and explain this whole situation. Then we need to see the lawyer that the letter is addressed to, and see what he knows and about this whole, crazy thing."

"Okay boys, we've seen enough," instructed George. "And let's do like Uncle Chip said; close everything up like you did the last time you were here. We'll go home and see if we can make some sense out of all of this. I must say, Caleb, you've really brought a big mystery into our house and I hope for everyone's sake that everything turns out alright."

"Yeah, dad," Caleb said a bit unsurely, "We can do that." Then with a renewed sparkle in his voice he added, "But don't you think this is a great place? I think it has some great potential and I've been thinking hard about what we can do with this house if we really get to own it like the papers say."

"Son," George cautioned, "don't you dare be making plans for something that may end up being a farce. Lawyers may tell us that we've been trespassing and had no business believing what Mr. Timberlake wrote."

"Actually, it sounds like Mr. Timberlake had a lot of hatred for his family members; and it also sounds like he was a candidate for the funny farm!" George continued. "I think we'll follow Chip's advice. I'm going to call a lawyer friend of mine just as soon as I get back to the house. Then, on Monday, we'll see about calling on the lawyer to whom that letter is addressed."

"Whatever you advise, dad, that's what Josh and I want to do," replied Caleb. "We came home to see you because I knew that you would know the best way to handle all of this. You know what, dad?"

"No, Caleb, what do you want to tell me?"

"We had loads of fun running through this house solving the riddles, finding the clues, breaking codes, working puzzles and finding the hidden room. Gosh! It was so much fun! But the treasure isn't what we expected, so I'm glad I have you and Uncle Chip to rely on to see what kind of a treasure we're going to end up with, if any. Thanks, dad, for being there for us."

"Son, you make me proud. Let's get on home, your mother is probably wondering what's happened to all of us," and Josh's parents should be arriving soon to pick him up and take him home. Then he put his arm around Caleb and gave him a small squeeze and added, "We're going to have to let everyone in on this, and your mom's going to have a fit about you boys rambling around in this old house. All she's going to think about is that you could've gotten your selves hurt real bad. But, all mothers are that way, so let's go face the music together." They all started laughing as they climbed the stairway to the main floor.

Chip remarked, "I think you boys are braver than I was at your age. I would've been afraid that this old house was haunted. You couldn't have gotten me to come in here for any amount of treasure."

The four of them laughed and talked cheerfully about the adventure as they walked down the road to where the car was parked. Then they loaded up and headed for home.

Mom met them at the door and said to George, "What's going on here? When I left for the store you and Chip were watching a Braves game. When I come back there's a mess of papers and money on the dining room table and everyone is gone. How about filling me in on what's going on?"

CHAPTER THIRTEEN

FAMILY MEETING

Everyone went into the house and sat down in the living room. George was about to tell his wife what was going on when in walked Chip's wife with a questioning look on her face, followed by Joshua's parents.

"Good evening, folks," welcomed George. "C'mon in and have a seat. I was just about to tell an interesting story. I think you'll enjoy it also, so have a seat and make yourselves comfortable."

George began to relate to everyone the story of what the boys had been up too. Chip explained how he and Caleb had been digging up the ground and found what Chip thought was an old Coke bottle, and that he had told Caleb he could have it. Then George got out the items that the boys had found in the container. He even sent Caleb to his room to bring back the container for everyone to see.

"That's an old glass rolling pin." Caleb's mom said excitedly. "You know, Sandy, who lives across the street, has a collection of rolling pins and several of them are glass. I just bet she would like to ad this one to her collection." Then looking so sweetly at her son, she encouraged, "Caleb, she's been so nice to you every since we moved here so why don't you be a sweet boy, and offer to give it to her?"

"Wait a minute! I don't think we need to do anything with any of these items until I can talk to a lawyer and make sure Caleb's not intruded where he shouldn't have," said George very emphatically.

"Oh, oh, you're right, dear; I just don't know what came over me," said June. "I just saw that rolling pin and lost my thoughts for a few minutes. But you're right. We need to get to the bottom of this mystery."

"Now, then," George continued, "we have the container, its contents which include a letter from Mr. Timberlake, a map that shows how to get from Chip's place to The Timbers, floor plans for The Timbers, and a bunch of riddle clues. And I must commend both of these boys for solving the riddles and obtaining the clues they needed to obtain the so-called treasure."

"Okay, George," said Joshua's dad, "what do you plan to do now?"

"I thought we might examine the contents of this metal box that the boys brought home. They seem to think that nothing that they found was a real treasure. But you and I know better. Some of the things they found, if they get to keep them, are valuable to collectors. Some may be valuable just as they are, but we won't know until we examine them and talk to someone who knows the law concerning this kind of a mystery hunt."

"So, let's open the metal box!" exclaimed Joshua's dad.

Everyone gathered around the dining room table where the metal box had been sitting. "Okay, everyone," said Caleb's dad. "I believe that there are enough chairs so you all can have a seat. I'm going to stand up so that I can show everyone what I take out of the box."

George snapped the lid open and took out a letter. "This letter is addressed to Robert C. Copeland, Esquire, Attorney, 1800 North Jackson Street, Tullahoma, Tennessee. It must have been written before zip codes, because there's not one on the letter. There is also a deed to The Timbers with a note that says it now belongs to the bearer of this letter. "

Next George removed two bundles of bills, which contained hundreds, fifties, twenties, tens, and a couple of fives. He stacked the bills and counted them. Then he announced, "Looks like there are two thousand dollars here. That doesn't seem like much today; however, these are all gold and silver certificates so they're worth more than their face value."

"Dad, what's a gold and silver certificate?" quizzed Caleb.

"You see, Caleb and Josh, when my dad, and granddad were young men every paper dollar bill had to be backed by silver or gold. Look here at this fifty dollar bill. See this gold seal right here?" he said as he pointed. "I want you to read out loud what it says."

Caleb looked at the bill and then said, "Dad, this doesn't even look like real money. Look what it says over here in the corner in big letters. 'THE NORTH WESTERN NATIONAL BANK OF MINNEAPOLIS MINNESOTA will pay to the bearer on demand FIFTY DOLLARS.' And then over that seal it says, 'Redeemable in lawful money of the United States at United States Treasury or at the bank of issue.' I've never, ever seen any money that looked like this stuff does."

"No," replied his father, "and you won't unless a collector has some because they quit producing gold and silver certificates." Then George went on to say, "If you had one of those bills back in 1930, you could have taken it to a bank and demanded that they give you fifty dollars worth of gold, because this is a gold certificate. If you had a bill with a silver seal on it, you could demand silver bullion for it. So, you see, these bills are worth a lot to a collector. I would say that this is a mighty good find."

George then brought out the rest of the papers. Looking them over, he said, "Hey, fellows you've a windfall here. These are all stock certificates in different denominations. Look here; there are stocks from Boeing, General Electric, General Mills, Shell Oil, Standard Oil, Lockheed, J.T. Baker Chemicals, Proctor and Gamble, Sears, Roebuck & Company, J.P. Morgan, Kroger's, Piggly Wiggly, and Coca Cola."

After studying the stock certificates for a moment or two, George explained, "I'm not sure when these were bought, but most of them are worth a pretty penny on the market today. Guys, if you get to keep these, you're going to be rich, very rich!"

The boys started shrieking and jumping up and down. "Wow, and we thought we hadn't found a treasure but we have! Hurray, hurray!" Even the adults were excited now.

"George, I think its time for you to call that lawyer friend of yours." said Joshua's dad. "We need to find out if these kids get to keep this stuff or if we have to locate the owners."

"You're right," said George excitedly, "so why don't all of you just sit and visit while I make a phone call or two. Honey, why don't you get everyone something to drink," he said to his wife as he headed toward the back of the house.

George went into his bedroom and closed the door, then picked up the phone and called his friend William Marks. After exchanging greetings with the lawyer, George began to relate the boys' adventure with the buried treasure and secret clues. Laughingly George continued, "The boys had a crazy time locating the actual treasure, but they did succeed! Now we're in a quandary about the legality of it all. Can the boys keep what they've found since it was actually hidden in an old house? The bottle Caleb found contained a letter that is notarized and gives them the privilege of owning everything they find. But it was notarized back in 1959, so how legal can it be now?"

"George," said the voice on the other end of the phone, "slow down a bit! Did you find anything else that I need to know about?"

"Yeah, Will--a hidden room full of antique clocks, collections of stamps and coins, a metal box containing $2,000 dollars in old currency, a deed to The Timbers, a bunch of stock certificates and a letter addressed to Robert C. Copeland, Esquire."

Laughing quite jovially Will said, "George, I would say that you've got yourself a challenging task ahead of you. I think I can help you out, but first I need to look at all of the stuff you're talking about. I'll tell you what, I'm eating my dinner right now, so give me time to finish and then I'll drive over and see if I can give you some advice." Laughing again, he said, "Your boy has really gotten himself quite a treasure if it's all legit. I'm looking forward to meeting this young man. See you in a little while."

George sat on the side of the bed for a few moments, gathering his thoughts. Then he prayed, "Lord, God Almighty, I praise your name and I thank you for all that we have. Father, I come to you now, asking that you put a wall of protection around Caleb and Josh. Lord, if this should be a legitimate treasure and the boys receive it, please give them the wisdom to use it wisely. Give all of us parents a calmness about everything and give us the wisdom to guide the boys in the right direction. Father, you and you alone know what is true and right. So I'm placing this entire situation into your hands. And I ask all of these things in the precious name of your son Jesus Christ. Amen."

With that prayer still on his heart, George joined the others in the dining room. "Folks," he said, "I've just spoken with William Marks who is a lawyer that handles wills, and such. And I think what we're dealing with here will fall somewhere in his field of the law, so I've asked him to come over tonight to look at all of this and advise us as to the next step we should take."

"What time will he be here?" enquired Josh's father.

"Edward," George said, "it will be late. So how about everybody goin' home and getting' some rest? Tomorrow, after church, everyone c'mon over here and we'll fix some sandwiches and talk about it all. Is that satisfactory with everyone?"

"Yeah, that works for me." said Edward with a yawn. "Get your stuff, Josh, and put it in the car. Come on, honey, let's get home and get some dinner."

As josh and his parents were leaving, Caleb ran to the door and called, "Night Josh, I'll see you at church tomorrow."

"Sure," Josh replied with a yawn, "tomorrow we'll get some answers, I hope. Goodnight, and be sure to keep all of our stuff safe."

"You don't have to worry about that. My dad will take care of everything now, so it will all be okay!" Then Caleb turned around to his mother and said, "I'm so tired. Can I just have a sandwich and some milk? Then I think I'll take a bath and go to bed."

"Yes, I'll fix you a sandwich, but don't you want to be up when Will comes over to check everything out?"

"Nope, I don't need to worry about it; dad will take care of it."

CHAPTER FOURTEEN

IT'S UP TO THE LAWYERS

Later that evening Attorney Marks arrived at the house where Caleb and his family lived.

"C'mon in here, Will," said George. "I don't know when I've been so glad to see a lawyer."

"Now, George, you don't think we lawyers are the bad guys, do you?" questioned William.

"No, of course not!" he said as he shook Will's hand. "But, most times you need a lawyer; you have to think you're in deep trouble. And if you need a lawyer it's going to cost you a bundle, no matter what. However," he continued, "you my friend are in my opinion one of the most honest men, and honest lawyers around." And then he injected, "That's why I called you before talking with anyone else. So come over here to the table and let's inspect these items."

The two men went to the dining room table and began sorting through all of the items in the box. Mr. Marks carefully pored over the documents that were in the container that Caleb found. Then with a big grin on his face he said, "George, we can start with this document right here. This notarized letter can be verified very easily."

"Even with it being that old?" exclaimed George.

"Yes. Age has nothing to do with it. You see, the law states that when a notary affixes their seal to a document, they are responsible for registering that information with the courthouse. These registrations are kept on file for times just like these, when a notary's stamp needs to be verified."

Then he turned the letter around and pointed to the seal that had been embossed in the paper. "Notice that here in the middle of this seal is a number that belongs to only one notary. All I have to do is go over to the courthouse in Manchester on Monday morning and ask them to look up Ms. Grime's registration. If she witnessed a document for Jacob Timberlake on September 16, 1959, we will have the proof that this is a real and legal document."

"Wow," George said with a gasp of disbelief, "just like that we'll know if the kids have a claim to all they've found!"

"Whoa, George," Will, replied calmly, "all I said is we will know if this document is for real." Then he continued, "Just because this one document is real doesn't mean that the boys have anything except what was in the container."

The lawyer shuffled through the papers in the box and studied them more closely. He also examined all of the currency and then examined the envelope that was addressed to Robert C. Copeland, Esquire.

"I can tell you this," he said to George, "these stock certificates are the real thing and are worth a lot of money. You've already noted that all of this currency is illegal to use because the government recalled all of their gold and silver certificates years ago. The only value that they might have is to numismatics. But since this currency has been hidden for a long time, the government might allow you to exchange it for today's currency. That is something that I will have to check. I've never had a case like this one. That is, if you are planning to hire me to represent the boys, should they have to go to court?"

"Well," said George, dumbfounded, "I really just wanted your opinion about what we have here and what to do next. I never thought about the boys having to go to court or for them even needing a lawyer."

"George," said Will in a friendly tone, "I hope you don't have to go to court. And maybe this will all be a lot easier than it first appears. But, you had better be ready for the worst. And, if you want, I'll be willing to help you and hopefully keep the boys from having to make a court appearance."

"Looks like we're between a rock and a hard place," George sighed. "How much is it going to cost us?"

"For something like this, most lawyers would take the case for thirty-three and a third percent of the monetary outcome of what the boys are entitled to. But, since we're such good friends and because I'm very interested in how this little venture is going to turn out for the boys, I think I'm going to offer my services for ten percent. And if they don't have to go to court but just need some papers processed, you pay the fees and my services are free. Does that sound fair to you?"

"More than fair," George replied with great relief. "But I do feel like it would only be fair for me to talk this over with the family and with Edward, that's Josh's dad. I want everyone to be in agreement. Is that okay with you?"

"Let's just make this a gentleman's agreement. You shake my hand, and we have an agreement, provided Edward doesn't object," said Will, as he extended his hand to George. The two men shook hands and chuckled.

Then George looked at all of the items on the table once more and shook his head. "Will, where do we even start to sort this puzzle out?"

"That, my friend, is why you need a lawyer. And the first place we go on Monday is to the courthouse in Manchester. Once we've verified the registration of this document, then we need to go see this other lawyer. This, by the way, isn't going to be easy."

"What?" said a surprised George. "Why isn't it going to be easy? All you have to do is call his office and make an appointment."

"If he were still alive, we could do that. But he passed away about eight years ago. However, he had a son, and I'm going to go home and see if I can find out how to get in touch with him," Marks replied, hoping to make George feel less anxious about everything.

"If he took over his dad's practice, he can act in his dad's place. That is, he can read the letter and he may already have some insight into what all of this is about. Mr. Timberlake may have been a regular client of Mr. Copeland and therefore the Copelands may already posses' other documents that will prove what rights the boys have to everything they've found."

"Whew, this is getting more and more complicated," said George as he sank into a chair. He rubbed his face with his hands and sighed, "This is too much to deal with any more tonight. Give me some time to talk with the family tomorrow, and then I'll get back with you, Will."

The lawyer turned around and started toward the door, when George got up and tapped him on the shoulder. As he turned around George said, "I really appreciate you taking the time to come by here tonight and look at all of this. You've already given me some good advice, and I do believe we'll be putting you on the case. But I just want to get a consensus of opinion from everyone who is involved with this. You do understand that it's not just my call?"

"Sure, George, I understand. Now you have a good night's rest and call me on Monday to let me know what your family decides to do." He patted George on the back and said, "Don't worry about the boys, they were innocently following directions. I don't think that any court would want to jail them for trespassing. But, they may not get to keep what they found. We'll just have to wait and see what we can find out. Now, friend, get a good night's rest."

George walked Will out to his car and said good night. Then he returned to the house, turned out the lights and joined his wife in the bedroom. "Dear," he said, "from what Will just explained to me, we're going to have our own adventure trying to find out if the boys get to keep all that they've found. Seeing if all of this is legal or not."

"George," June said, "all we can do is put it in the Lord's hands and not worry about it. So what if the boys don't get to keep what they found? They had fun finding it, didn't they? So I would say no matter what, Caleb and Josh will be happy. They didn't have anything before they started, so they're losing nothing."

George just stared in disbelief, as he listened to what his wife was saying. "You may take it that way, but I think Caleb has his heart set on acquiring this treasure. He's already been planning what he can do with it. And, I just bet that Josh has been making plans, too."

"Oh, for land sakes, George," June said with a snap, "let's get some rest. We can talk about this tomorrow. But I don't want to hear a word about any of this until after church and lunch. Then you can talk to your heart's content. Now, get in this bed and let's get some sleep, I'm tired and you should be, too."

CHAPTER FIFTEEN

AFTER LUNCH ON SUNDAY

Immediately after church Caleb and his family went home. Once in the house his mother and two sisters started preparing lunch for everyone, and Caleb went to his bedroom to change into some more comfortable clothes.

Caleb was having a hard time not thinking about The Timbers and what he could do with the house if he and Josh actually got to keep it, in accordance with the instructions Jacob Timberlake had left. Once he had his clothes changed, he laid back on his bed to dream some more about the possibilities.

"Man, oh man," he thought, "what a great hangout that basement would make for us kids. With a two lane bowling alley and those two billiard tables, we could have some team competition. We could set up a refreshment stand near the stairwell with some tables and chairs." With more and more excitement his mind was running wild with ideas. "Wouldn't it be neat to clear out that wine cellar and make it into a laser tag facility?"

Caleb's thought process was interrupted by knocks on his door and the voice of his oldest sister, Macula, chiding him, "Hey, boy, you hiding from the rest of the family? Are you too shy to show your face to your cousin? Hey, guy, you want me to serve the celebrity his meal in his room?"

Caleb grabbed the door and ripped it open. "No! Besides, Macula I didn't know Josh was here, so excuse me while I go greet my guest," he said snidely, and then they both broke out laughing.

"Dad told me to come and get you because everyone was here, and he thought maybe you had fallen asleep," she said with a pleasant tone.

"Who could sleep?" Caleb said. "All I can do is think, think and think, of all the things Josh and I found at The Timbers and make plans for using the grounds."

"Dad told you not to make any plans till he finds out where everything stands legally," she warned.

"Sis, have you ever tried NOT to think about something?" he sighed.

"Yeah, you're right, the more you try to stop the more you think about it," she said as she patted him on the back. "I really sympathize with you and Josh. But, I'm proud of the way you decided to come home and tell Dad and Uncle Chip about everything and then ask for their help. Most kids would have been afraid to tell their parents."

"Well, Dad is special," he said with a beaming smile on his face. "He has never punished me except when I deserved it. He always takes time to explain things - even my wrongdoings. I just know that he is always going to help me, so why shouldn't I come home and tell him the whole story and then ask him to help me." Caleb looked up at his sister and said, "We're lucky to have such a good, God-fearing man for our dad. Maybe we need to tell him more often what he means to us."

"Caleb," she said with a twinkle in her eye, "for a little brother you sure are smart. I love you to death and I'm going to miss you this year while I'm away at college. But don't you dare change from the person you are, 'cause you're great in my book."

The two of them went down the hallway toward the front of the house. Caleb heard Josh's voice and went running into the den. "Hey, Josh, why didn't you c'mon back to my room when you got here?"

Rolling his eyes and nodding his head toward his dad. Josh explained, "Dad wanted me to stay right here with him until your dad explained what that lawyer had to say."

"Okay," Caleb said, "let's sit right here at the table by the window. We can talk and we're in full view of everyone. How's about it, cuz?"

"Hey, dad," said Joshua, "is it all right if Caleb and I sit here by the window and talk while we're waiting for lunch?"

"You just stay put," Edward said sternly, "I want you to be where I can get you to answer some questions for me when the time comes. Sitting by the window is okay, but stay there and don't you move from there 'til I tell you to. Do you understand me?"

The boys looked at each other, grimaced and shrugged their shoulders. "Sure," they said in unison, "we'll be right here."

As the boys began talking to each other, Edward walked over to George and asked, "When are we going to get this show on the road?"

"Ed, what are you talking about?" said George with a quizzical look on his face.

"I want to know when you're going to start filling us in on what you and that lawyer talked about last night," Edward said with a snarl in his voice. "Is my kid going to be in trouble with the law? Is this high jinx they were on just a farce?" "I didn't sleep a wink last night, so I think it's about time that you tell the rest of us just what is really going on!"

George turned to Ed, placed his arm around his shoulder and said, "Ed, calm down, will, ya? Everything is under control, and I'm going to explain things when everyone gets here and after everyone has eaten."

Looking sternly around the room, Ed said, "Looks like everyone's here to me. And who cares about eating. I want to get to the bottom of this, right now!"

"Ed," George said in a calm voice, "Chip and his family haven't arrived yet."

"Chip and his family," he retorted. "What does Chip have to do with any of this? It's Caleb and Josh that you should be concerned about."

"Ed, we're going to handle this in a fair and compassionate manor," George stated in a matter-of-fact tone. "Caleb did find the container on Chip's property and Chip is also curious about what's going to happen. And even if he gave the container to Caleb, he still has the right to repossess it if he so wishes. So, we will wait till they arrive and we will sit down and have a quiet mealtime before I explain to everyone what Will pointed out to me last night." With a somber smile, George patted Ed on the back and offered him the best chair in the den.

In a few minutes the back door flew open and there stood Chip with his baby cuddled up in his arms and his two-year old clinging to his leg. Caleb's mother rushed over to take the baby and began playing with her. Chip reached down and picked up the toddler. Then he said, "Millie's on her way. Sorry folks, but sometimes these little ones slow us down a bit. But, we're here now!"

George and Chip shook hands and began a conversational rerun of yesterday's baseball game between the Braves and the Giants. Meanwhile, a very fidgety, stone-faced Ed sat in the chair and nervously thumped his fingers on the arm rest. During this time, the women hugged, and chattered away as they sat the food on the table. Of course, Caleb and Josh were quietly chatting about plans for the treasures they hoped to acquire.

"Food's ready," called out Caleb's mom.

"About time," grumbled Edward.

"C'mon folks," said George cheerfully. "Let's gather around in a circle and take a moment to thank the Lord for the blessings of the day."

Everyone got up and stood in a circle in the kitchen, and Caleb reached out and held hands with his sister and Josh. Pretty soon everyone had followed his lead and everyone was holding hands with their heads bowed in reverence. "Son," George said softly, "why don't you lead us in this time of thanksgiving."

"Yes, sir," he said respectfully. Then with his head bowed and eyes closed he said, "Heavenly Father, thank you for the sunshine you brought us this day. Thank you for the wonderful family that you have blessed Josh and me with. Father, we have a lot of decisions to make and we ask you to guide us, and to guide my Dad in doing what is right about Mr. Timberlake's property. I know he said who ever found it could keep it, but I don't want to cause anybody any heartache. Bless the food that has been prepared; bless the hands of those who prepared it. May it strengthen and nourish our bodies. Help us to grow spiritually stronger every day. Amen."

George looked up, and with a twinkle in his eye, he looked at Caleb and said, "Thanks, son. Now, everyone, let's eat!"

Everyone got their plates fixed and sat around in various places in the house, and began eating their lunch. They all appeared to be enjoying themselves. Everyone, that is, except Ed. Ed was keeping a watchful eye on Josh, and was getting more fidgety by the moment. To be exact, Ed looked like he was about to blow up, when George walked over and with a calm voice said, "Ed, you need to simmer down and enjoy yourself. We're just about finished, and I'll get started with the meeting in just a few more minutes. Okay?"

"Yeah," said Ed under his breath. "I don't think this family ever gets excited about anything. Here I'm sittin' on pins and needles, while they laugh and carry on like it's a celebration of some sort."

Soon the jovial mealtime came to an end. George collected all of the materials that the boys had found and put them on the table. Then he asked that everyone gather in the living room. Everyone sat comfortably, even if some were sitting on the floor. George wanted everyone seated where they could see and hear him and also see the items that were on the table.

"William Marks, Attorney at Law," George began, "and I had a long and informative discussion about all of these items and instructions. The good news is that the first letter the boys found was notarized and by law the notarized document had to be registered by the notary with the courthouse. So, Will says, if we want him to represent the boys, he would be glad to go over to the courthouse in Manchester and check to see if and when the note was registered. This would prove whether or not this is a legal document."

There was a long silence in the room. Then Edward blurted out, "What do we need him for? Any idiot could go to the courthouse and check that information out. It's a matter of public record." Scornfully he continued, "Just another lawyer trying to milk every dollar they can out of you!"

"Hold on, Ed," George said firmly. "That's not all. I found out that this other letter that was addressed to lawyer Copeland may have the proof we need that the boys can keep everything. However, he passed away eight years ago. So now we have to deal with his son, IF his son knows about the case and can help us."

"Drats," snarled Ed, "don't you have any good news for us?"

"Yes, Ed, but let me first explain some of the complications of this situation. And then I'll explain the good aspects."

"I hear ya," grumbled Ed, "just hurry up and get to the good stuff, will ya?"

"Josh and Caleb," George called, as he motioned to them to come over and stand beside him. "Boys, we have a decision to make here with regards to this whole adventure of yours. I feel that since the treasure may or may not belong to you, and because you did all of the work in locating it, then you should make the decision on what I'm about to reveal to everyone. So, please, listen closely."

"Whoa, George," Ed shouted as he jumped to his feet. "No son of mine is going to make any kind of decision about anything. I'm the one who makes the decisions in this family."

Once more in a stern, soft voice George instructed Ed to sit down and hear him out. "Boys," George went on to say, "even if you have the rights to these items, we may still have to go to court. If we go to court we need the type of lawyer that Mr. Marks is. He is trained in dealing with wills, estates, deeds, trusts and real estate. Therefore, Mr. Marks would be a good person to represent you to the courts and he is willing to do all of the investigating for us. All you have to do is decided if you would like him to represent you."

"And what kind of an 'arm and leg' fee is he wanting to charge these kids?" snapped Edward.

"Actually, Ed, he has made a more than fair offer. If it is just processing papers, the boys pay the fees, his service is free. If it becomes a court case and successful, the boys will owe him one tenth of the value of the estate. If he is unsuccessful, they will owe him nothing."

"Gyp, that's all any lawyer is," snarled Ed. "He's probably taking advantage of them, and you call him a friend?"

"Ed, I'm losing my patience with you," snapped George.

"Yeah," chimed in Chip, "me, too. What's your problem? These boys did a great job of finding this stuff. They deserve all of the credit for it and I personally want to see them get every bit of it just like the old fellow has it written out. So, why don't you quit all the gruff and groan and rejoice with the boys and let them decide what they want to do with the treasure they've worked so hard for."

"Dear," said Josh's mom, "Chip and George is right. Let's listen to the boys and back them up. I...a...hmmm...what I mean to say is, they didn't have anything before they started, so if they lose it, they've lost nothing." Then with a beaming smile she looked at Josh and said, "Go on, son, listen to Uncle George, you and Caleb put your heads together and decide what you want to do. I'm in your corner!"

"Let me explain something to you, Ed," George said. "Typically, in this type of legal action, lawyers take the case for thirty-three and a third percent of the judgment gain. Will, as a favor to the boys, is willing to take the case for ten percent. Now that sounds more than fair to me." Then George looked at the boys and went on to say, "If, and I must emphasize the IF, the estate is yours, you will in all probability have to go through probate and might have to pay some inheritance tax. And that means you might have to cash in some of these stock certificates in order to have money to pay the taxes."

As the boys stood there beside him, looking blankly at each other, George got down on his knees beside them and said gently, "Guys, it's your call. Do you want me to get William Marks to represent you?"

"Time out!" shouted Caleb. "I think Josh and I need to go to my room - by ourselves – and sort this out. All of you know a lot about the law, we don't. Besides, Uncle Ed doesn't seem to be happy about any of this and I know that is sort of upsetting to Josh. So I think all of you need to give us a break." Then looking quizzically at his dad Caleb said, "Is that okay, dad?"

"Wise words from a child," said George with a grin. "You boys take all the time you want. The rest of us are going to have some more desserts, if that's all right with you ladies."

While the men worked at reasoning with Ed, the boys went back to Caleb's room. There they flopped down on the bed and thought. Caleb was the first to break the silence.

"I don't know how you feel about all of this, but it sounds like the plan Mr. Marks and Dad talked about is the answer to our problems. I think your mom said it best; we don't really have anything to lose, 'cause if we lose in court Mr. Marks isn't going to charge us anything. If we win, we can cash in those stock certificates."

"Caleb," sighed Josh, "I just knew when I tagged along with you on this so called adventure of yours; I was going to get in some sort of trouble. My dad has been grumbling ever since we showed him this stuff."

"What's he so upset about?" Caleb questioned. "We haven't done anything bad."

Josh pounded the bed with his fist and said, "All he thinks about is that some way or another he's going to have to lay out a bunch of money for what we've done. You know how tight money is in our house. I just don't want him angry and upset."

"I'm sorry," said Caleb as he patted Josh on the back. "I just wanted to have some fun before the summer's end. I had no idea finding a treasure would cause such an uproar. Tell me," Caleb asked, "do you feel like it would be good for us to hire Mr. Marks to help us?"

"Yeah," Josh replied, "your dad made it sound like that would be best. If it's the best offer, then let's go for it!"

"Good for you," Caleb cheered. "See, you can make good decisions."

Caleb jumped up, grabbed Josh and the two of them danced around the bedroom, hollering, cheering and making quite a ruckus. Their jubilance spilled over into the rest of the house, and in a moment three sisters were banging on the door. "Have you guys flipped your lids," they laughed.

"No," the boys chorused from inside the room. Then Caleb opened the door and said decisively, "We are about to make an announcement. So, why don't you girls go proclaim our grand entrance?"

Giggling as they went, the girls ran to the living room where they proclaimed to all who were present, "The family royalty, Prince Caleb and Prince Joshua, will presently enter the room with a royal decree. Ladies and Gentlemen, please stand until they have entered the room and sat down."

Everyone, except Ed, joined in the fun. They all stood up as the boys entered the room and took adjoining seats at the table. "Hear ye, hear ye, family members," proclaimed Caleb in a melodramatic manner. "Prince Josh and I have made a decision and we wish to make the announcement together." With that the boys stood up grabbed adjoining hands and lifting them in the air like champions they loudly proclaimed, "Call Mr. Marks to represent us!"

Everyone congratulated them and George went to the phone to call the Lawyer. Marks outlined his plan to George, and made arrangements to get back with the family later in the week when he knew more about the mysterious happening with The Timbers.

The boys were happy, most of the adults were happy, and Caleb looked up at George and said, "Dad, I just knew that you would know the right thing to do. Thanks for helping us out."

CHAPTER SIXTEEN
WHO GETS THE ESTATE?

Early Tuesday morning, George received a call from the attorney about the progress of the investigation into the Jacob Timberlake Estate. "George," he said cheerfully, "I've got some good news. We did find records indicating that the note that Caleb found in the container was indeed registered and is the original, certified document."

"Great," said George, "the boys do have rightful claims to the estate, then!"

"Not so fast," said Will in a more somber tone, "this only means that they had the right to follow the directions and locate the items that Mr. Timberlake hid from his family. But whether or not the boys are allowed to keep these items is an entirely different matter."

George scratched his head, and began to pace the floor as he continued their phone conversation. "What am I to tell the boys? I don't want to lift their hopes only to have everything come crashing down later on. Come, tell me, Will, where do we go from here?"

"I just knew you would ask me that question, so before I called you I got in touch with Mr. Copeland's office. You and I have an appointment with him at 1:00 pm tomorrow. Do you think you can make that meeting?"

"This is important to Caleb and Josh, so I will make it to the meeting even if I have to cancel some other appointments. These boys are excited about the prospects of getting the house and the other items they found. So, I am praying that their wish comes true."

"George, it might be a good idea to hold off telling them anything until you and I have a chance to talk with Mr. Copeland," he pointed out. "That way they won't get all excited before the final part of the investigation is completed. After all, if Mr. Copeland isn't aware of Jacob Timberlake's Estate, he may have to spend some time digging into his father's old records in order to give us some answers. Depending on his work load, that could take from weeks to a year. And, having sons of my own, I know how impatient they can get about having to wait on anything," he snickered. "Especially if what they're waiting on is the answer to a question!"

George laughed goodheartedly, and agreed with Will. When Caleb came in and asked, "Has Mr. Marks got an answer for us yet?" George sat him down for a long talk. He explained that legal matters, especially when things had to be investigated, usually weren't completed in a day's time. He told Caleb that he and Mr. Marks had an appointment scheduled for the next day with Mr. Copeland, but just because they had an appointment, didn't mean they would find all of the answers tomorrow.

"Caleb," George said softly, "this is the hardest part. You and Josh are going to have to show patience. And patience is a virtue that most boys your age don't have. Learning to have patience is part of the growing up process. So, both of you have an opportunity here to mature a little more."

"Great," Caleb spouted cheerfully. "But Dad, I just can't stop thinking about what we can do with all of that stuff. I mean, well, my mind just keeps making plans even when I tell it to stop," he said sadly. Then he shrugged his shoulders, looked up sort of sheepishly at his father and said, "I think I can wait patiently for an answer from Mr. Marks, but I can't stop planning things. Is it okay to just think about 'what if'?"

George laughed and reached out, grabbed Caleb up in his arms and gave him a big hug. "Son, you just do all the planning you want. Remember," he cautioned, "that your dreams may not come true. But, I wouldn't stop you from dreaming for anything in the world."

Just then the phone rang and Caleb went to answer it. "Oh, hi, Josh, has your dad gotten any happier?"

"Yes," Josh said, "Mom explained everything again when we got home. I think Mom convinced him that Mr. Marks is going to treat us honestly and work hard to find the answers to all of the questions we have. I was calling to see if Mr. Marks has found out anything yet.

"No, Mr. Marks hasn't gotten an answer for us yet. But he and my dad have an appointment with Mr. Copeland tomorrow. So maybe we'll have some news then," said Caleb in a very business-like manner. "Dad said we need to learn to have patience, that patience was the virtue of a mature man. So, we just need to wait and see what they find out. When Dad knows something, he'll tell us."

"Well, that sounds just great," Josh growled. But how am I going to teach my dad patience? Every time I turn around he wants me to call your house and see what's going on with the investigation. My dad is driving me crazy!"

"I've got an idea," Caleb responded. "Why don't you have your dad call mine tonight? Then my dad can explain what's going on and you won't have to worry about it. And you know my dad is great when it comes to explaining things."

"Yeah," Josh said gleefully, "and maybe he can talk some of the anger out of him. He's still upset about us hiring Mr. Marks to help us. He thinks we're being robbed."

"Do you think we're being robbed? Do you think we did the right thing by letting him represent us?" questioned Caleb. "You know, I didn't force you into agreeing with me. I just thought that my dad was guiding us in the right direction."

There was dead silence on the phone. Caleb stood there and held the receiver for a few minutes more and then he said softly, "Josh…Josh, are you still there?"

"Yeah," replied Joshua with a sad voice. "I'm so confused. Everything yesterday seemed so clear. But, you just don't know my dad. He's been fussing all night long, and the more he fusses the more, unsure I become about our decision. But, well, hmm," he sighed, "I guess I'm going to stick with the decision we made. You're just lucky to have a dad that sees things so clearly."

"Yeah, I know," Caleb said with a big grin on his face.

"I've got to go do some chores before I get in trouble," Josh said. "Call me when you have some news. For now I'm going to try to stop thinking about all of this fussin.' Bye."

The next day Will and George went to the law offices of Copeland, Harwell and Livingston. There they met with Charles Copeland, the son of the late Robert C. Copeland. After greetings and introductions were completed the men sat down at a table and Will opened his briefcase and took out the papers that Caleb had found in the container as well as those that were in the metal box, including the letter addressed to Robert C. Copeland.

Will and George went into great detail explaining what happened and how the boys came into possession of everything. Will also explained about his findings at the courthouse in Manchester.

"Well, well," Charles Copeland laughed. "This is quite a story, and I'm sure it was a great adventure for the boys." Stroking his chin, and seeming to have drifted off into another world, Mr. Copeland just sat there nodding his head and grinning from ear to ear. This made Will and George feel a little bit uneasy.

"What's the matter," George blurted out, "do you think this is some sort of joke?"

"Ahhh," Mr. Copeland sighed. "No indeed," he said while shaking his head and scratching his ear, "…no, I was just remembering Jacob Timberlake. You see, he and my dad were very good friends. Old Jacob grew up with great work ethics and having been poor most of his life, he worked very hard to build a great business. Or maybe I had better say, many businesses, that in turn prospered, and brought him a great fortune. However, he could never instill those work ethics in his offspring. So in frustration he vowed that they would never get their hands on those things he valued most in life. He would rather a complete stranger had them than to allow his spoiled children to posses them."

"So, what happened with his estate after he died?" asked Will.

"He was a very intelligent man. And he knew that his family would probably contest his will, so he conspired with my father to keep this from happening. After his death, as I remember, Dad gathered the family in the parlor of the estate and read the will to them. What a sight that was!" he exclaimed. "I was just a teenager then and since I had expressed an interest in taking up law as my major in college, dad let me sit in on the reading."

"First, the Mrs. was given the privilege of living at *The Timbers* estate, until such time as she passed away. Each of the four children was given a small trust fund to sustain them with the basics of life. And then Mr. Timberlake had included the statement: *With the hope that you will be encouraged to get out and build a fortune for yourselves just as I did.*"

"Now here is the rough part that Dad had to deal with," said Mr. Copeland with a small chuckle. "The old boy had Dad add this statement to his will: *Being of sound mind at the writing of this will, I, Jacob Timberlake, do bestow up on that person, whoever they may be, my home at The Timbers, and whatever items they have acquired through my instructions to them. All of these things will become their legal possessions upon presenting the proper credentials to the Copeland Law Offices. Not ANY of my estate, nor any item I have listed for Mr. Copeland, my attorney, will ever be possessed by my offspring. I have made sure that you will not starve to death, but it's time that you left the nest and made your own way in this world.'"*

"I have to ask," said George, "did his children contest the will?"

"They wanted to, but Jacob was a sly person to deal with. You see, he also had a legal agreement drawn up that said whoever tried to contest the will would lose their trust fund and if they lost the court battle, which he assured them that they would, they would have nothing."

"Okay," said Will, "how did he set it up for someone to claim the estate?"

"I really didn't know anything about how Dad and Jacob were going to decide who was to get his estate. But, I notice you have a letter here addressed to dad. How about me taking a look at it and maybe it will shed some light on this matter."

Mr. Copeland opened the aged envelope and began reading the letter.

> "Robert, my friend, as we planned, if you are reading this letter then you know that someone found the clues I left for obtaining the possessions of my estate, my collections, and my stock certificates. I also placed some cash in my cash box to help cover any further expenses you may incur while placing all these things into the possession of the finder.
>
> I know, without a doubt, that whoever takes the time to search out the answers to my riddles and seek the reward, must be someone who has great incentive to

achieve much in life and that person is due this just reward. Tell this person, for me, that I have great respect for anyone who has the drive and ingenuity to have conquered this task. I purposely made it long and difficult. This was to test their patience and endurance. And if they are standing before you now, they have endured the test and deserve the reward, so please, with my blessing, present them with the keys to my house. And sign over the deed, which they have in the box, to them. As a reminder to you, we did set up a trust fund to keep the taxes paid up on this property forever. So be sure to inform them of that arrangement."

"Then," Mr. Copeland, concluded, "he finished by signing it, 'respectfully yours, Jacob Timberlake.'"

"So, Charles," asked Will, "do we, or should I say do the boys, need to go before a probate court in order to get all of this finalized?"

"I'll check on that," the lawyer said, "but because of the structure of the law back then, when the original 'will' was filed with the courthouse, there was no need to go to probate if you had a properly filed 'will.' And this would mean that the 'will' falls under that time period."

"So, what else do we need to do?" questioned George.

"Not much," explained Mr. Copeland. "Just bring the boys down here to my office so that they can sign some papers. And because they are minors, I will need an adult to represent each of them and co-sign the legal contracts. Then leave the rest to Mr. Marks and me. You will have a few fees to pay for processing the papers. Then it's all done."

"But, I have to tell you that I'm excited about the probability of meeting the boys," he said with a chuckle. "I hope they will take the time to tell me the whole story of how they got started looking for this stash and how they figured the answers to the riddles. What an adventure they must have had! Makes me a little envious of them," he laughed.

After a few moments of exchanging laughter and small stories of childhood incidents the three men said their good-byes and made arrangements for the meeting with the boys. George couldn't get home fast enough to tell Caleb the good news.

Immediately, Caleb called Josh and the two of them celebrated with whoops and hollers over the phone. Then they made plans for Josh and his family to come over and have supper and discuss what they were going to do with the rewards of their labor.

CHAPTER SEVENTEEN
UNITED WE STAND

A week later Joshua came over to Caleb's house and the two boys were in the bedroom making plans for using what they had located at 'The Timbers'. As usual Caleb took charge of everything, and Josh agreed with whatever Caleb suggested. Finally it came to a point at which Josh realized that Caleb couldn't possibly do what he was talking about without some adult supervision.

"Caleb," said Josh emphatically, "you need to talk to your dad about this. And you need to talk to him about it now!"

Rolling his eyes and shaking his head Caleb conceded, "You're so right. Let's go." Caleb picked up the charts he had drawn and the sheets he had done his figuring on, and he and Josh went to the den to talk to George.

George was stretched out the full length of the sofa, snoring up a storm, with the book he had been reading flopped across his chest.

Caleb leaned over the back of the sofa and tapped his dad on the belly. "Dad, Dad, wake up. Please wake up, I need to talk to you."

George opened one eye and yawned, "Son, let me rest a little while longer, please."

"Dad, this is important. If it weren't important I wouldn't be waking you up." Caleb whined.

"Okay, you win," said George as he sat up. "What's so cotton pick'in important that it couldn't wait until I had my nap?"

"Josh and I have been working on plans for 'The Timbers' and Josh thinks we shouldn't go any further without you being in on the planning. And I'm beginning to realize that my cuz is a pretty smart fellow. So I want you to listen to our ideas, look at some figures I've jotted down, and look at some sketches I've made." Then with even more excitement in his voice he said, "And tell us how we can make this happen!"

"Well, I would say that you've got a fire lit under you," his dad laughed. "So, who wants to begin?"

Josh dropped his head and stammered, "Caleb always does a better job of explaining things so let him do it. I'll just chime in with the things he forgets to say if that's okay."

"Okay, shoot, Caleb!"

"Dad, you know there is no place in our town for kids to hang out and have fun."

"Okay, so what do you want to do about it?" challenged George.

"Josh and I have 'The Timbers' and the taxes are paid on it, and we have all of that money and those clocks, stamps, coins, and stocks."

"Right," said George. "But 'The Timbers' is in a terribly run-down condition."

"Yeah, Dad," said Caleb thoughtfully, "but look at my drawings." Caleb spread some drawings out on the floor. He had very meticulously drawn a recreation area in the basement of 'The Timbers'.

"See, we could have bowling, and the bowling lanes are in good shape, we just need to buy some pins and balls. We can fix the pool tables and have some dartboards set up over here," he said pointing to an area across from where the bowling lanes were located.

Then Josh piped in, "And over here we can set up a concession stand and some tables and chairs."

"And look, Dad," Caleb said excitedly, "we have to go all the way to Nashville to play Laser Tag…but if we clean out this wine cellar we could set up a Laser Tag there."

"Not a bad idea, son," said George. "But, do you think you could get the kids to go out there and use the facility? And what are your plans for the rest of the building?"

"Well," said Josh, "I think the first thing we need to do is to get some volunteers to go out there and help us to clean up that property. We need to get all of those bushes trimmed up. Fix that road that's going up to the house and for sure we need to get that gate all fixed up," he said emphatically. "Uncle George, do you think you could talk some of the kids from the youth group at church into coming over and giving us a hand with cleaning up this lot? If twelve or fifteen of us worked on it together, we could probably do it in a couple of Saturdays, don't you think?"

"You've got a good point there, Josh," George said with a smile. "I'll see what I can do about lighting a fire under some of those young people. But, what are you going to offer them in return?" he queried.

"I know what," yelled Caleb, "get us a fire permit and we'll have a bonfire with all the rubbish and we'll cook hotdogs, and roast marshmallows."

"Okay guys," George said with a twinkle in his eye. "So far I've heard about what Caleb wants to do with the basement and what Josh wants to do with the grounds. Is that all there is to your plans?"

"Shucks, no!" exclaimed Caleb. "After we get the grounds cleared, we want to have an area set up to play some basketball and another area to play baseball, and volley ball."

Then Josh pointed out, "Caleb has some more drawings and ideas for the building. Uncle George, you need to look at them, they're real neat."

"Well, show me whatcha got, Caleb," George prodded.

Rubbing his head, and then the back of his neck, Caleb reached down and laid out a drawing of the front of the building and said, "Now, I've been giving this a lot of thought ever since we thought we were going to get this building. I want it to be used by the community and to be a memorial to Mr. Timberlake. That basement is going to make a great recreational area for kids.

But, there are tons of books in the library. So I thought we could get them down, fix up the library, clean up the books and put them back and add more books so kids visiting out here could use the library." Catching his breath he went on, "and the living room is huge. It could be used for parties and dances. The dining room could be fixed up and be used for catered meals. The parlor could be fixed up and used for small gatherings. And there is a wonderful kitchen that just needs a little repair work."

"And what's this here that you've drawn in on each side of the front door?" George asked Caleb.

"Oh, those are elevators to get to the second and third floors. I plan on putting apartments on the second floor for the college students to rent. And on the third floor I have this great idea," he said, talking even more excitedly than ever, "part of the area will be a movie theatre and the other part will be a unique game room. I want to take all of the wine vats, cut the fronts off of them and place computers inside each one. The only kinds of games you can play are games that challenge the mind," he said with a twinkle in his eye and a big grin all over his face. "Isn't that neat?"

Scratching his chin and nodding his head, George just sits in silence for a long, long while. Then he said, "Boys, these are big plans, but I think they are worthy plans and I'm willing to help you try to achieve your goals. But, you need to know that it won't happen overnight."

"That's okay dad, if you'll just help us," shouted Caleb.

Joshua said, "I agree!"

CHAPTER EIGHTEEN
FOUR YEARS LATER

"Hey, Caleb," said Josh excitedly, "did you ever imagine in all your life that we would be so lucky in finding this place?"

"No," Caleb chuckled. "Don't think Uncle Chip or my Dad thought we would be so successful. We've provided a good, safe place for the kids to hang out, inexpensive apartments for college students, and we've managed to get a lot of adults involved in helping us do it."

"You know what I wish?" said Josh thoughtfully.

"No, what?" asked Caleb.

"I wish Mr. Timberlake were alive so we could thank him for the wonderful gift he has given to our community." Then after thinking for a few minutes he added, "Do you think his kids would appreciate knowing what we've done with their house? Or the story of how we even got the house?"

"Nah," said Caleb. "From what Mr. Copeland said they weren't interested in anything but money and themselves. I'm just thankful that Uncle Chip needed some help and that I found that container and our adventure ended with this beautiful center." With a big grin on his face, he said, "Cuz, give me a high five!"

The two boy jumped as high as they could, smacking their right hands together. As they settled to the ground again, they put their arms around each other's shoulders and marched through the shiny gates of 'The Timbers.'

ABOUT THE AUTHOR

Fran Johnson was born in Riverside, California but grew up in Las Vegas, Nevada. For the first four years of her life she spent much of her time with grown ups and in order to entertain herself she turned to fantasy. Her vivid imagination helped her to develop exciting stories to tell to her children and later to write in book form for her grandchildren. Her fifteen grandchildren have quickly grown up, so now she wants to share her tales with the children of the world. Presently she lives in Tullahoma TN with her husband, near one of her grandsons.

ABOUT THE ILLUSTRATOR

Francis Sargent was born and raised on the West Coast. From childhood, her only desire has been to become a known artist. She received her teaching degree from the University of Tennessee, and was a high school Graphic Arts instructor for many years.

Francis has studied under Steven Lesnic, Sunrise Studios, Las Vegas, Nevada; Rex Brandt, Blue Sky Studios, Newport, California; and Norma Dennison, Jackson State, Jackson, Tennessee. She works in a variety of media, watercolor being her favorite.

Printed in the United States
135664LV00004BA/1/P